# CHRISTMAS
## IN
# PORT CHANCE

D. E. MALONE

\* \* \*

With the holidays approaching, Sadie Wendell fights the melancholy of experiencing another Christmas alone. She loves caring for injured animals at her wildlife rehab center, but it doesn't fill the void she still feels years after a bitter divorce. Even taking on a new business partner to stave off money troubles isn't the distraction she needs. Then her partner's brother walks into the rescue in the midst of a squirrel catastrophe, turning Sadie's dismal holiday season upside down.

Hayes Kelley vows to make the best of being laid off from his job, and working alongside Sadie at Furever Friends Rescue while helping his sister recuperate might be an unexpected gift this holiday season. Trouble is, he's convinced Sadie feels his presence around the property is like finding coal in her stocking.

When a patron proposes a fundraiser for the center, Sadie reluctantly accepts Hayes' help. Can he convince her that their temporary partnership might be a chance to heal her heartbreak before his time runs out in Port Chance?

Christmas in Port Chance
Copyright © 2025 D.E. Malone
All rights reserved.
Cover designed by Red Leaf Book Design
Library of Congress Cataloging-in-Publication Data has been applied for

For exclusive content and book news, subscribe to D.E. Malone's *Welcome to the Sweet Life* newsletter.

*Chapter One*

When Sadie Wendell peered into her future ten years ago, she'd imagined packing school lunches for her children instead of preparing a mash for a baby squirrel at her wildlife rescue, Furever Friends.

At present, she had no children. Well, not the *human* kind anyway.

"One CUP coconut oil. A quarter cup NUTS."

Sadie recited the recipe for squirrel mash loudly enough to drown out the racket behind her, but it was futile. The intermittent thuds against the side of the plastic tub were frenzied enough that Sadie stopped measuring ingredients and whirled around.

"Seriously? I'm working as fast as I can."

The squirrel pressed its nose against one of the makeshift ventilation holes in the lid when Sadie came closer. It disappeared then resurfaced at another hole. "I'll get you nice and comfortable in another minute."

The tub wobbled on the countertop like it had a mind of its own—well, it kind of did—so she set it on the floor at her feet

1

so she could finish mixing up the mash. She dumped kibble into the blender along with the mash she'd mixed and turned on the machine. The blender pulverized the contents, making the utensils resting next to it on the counter dance with the vibrations. It even drowned out the chattering of one irritated squirrel, her newest patient. The squirrel was one of eleven she cared for at the moment. It was nearing the end of the fall baby season, so most of her squirrels were under three weeks old. It wore her to the bone, the round-the-clock feedings when they were this young.

She shut the blender off.

The squirrel churred, no doubt upset about being confined in the tub.

*Ahh, I know how you feel, kiddo.*

Sometimes, Sadie wanted the world to leave her alone, too.

The door to the shed opened behind her and in breezed her partner, Cara Ortega. She pushed the fur-lined hood from her head and ruffled the melting snowflakes from her honey-hued bangs.

"Everyone has been fed and watered. Pepper's enclosure still needs cleaning, so I'll do that, then head to town for the feed." Cara approached the box and peered through one of the holes. "She looks like she's in better spirits than she did an hour ago."

"Feisty, that's for sure." Sadie lifted the blender from the base. "Is it still snowing?"

"Not too much. It's disappearing as fast as it hits the ground."

Popping off the blender's lid, Sadie dumped the mixture into a small metal dish and set it inside the nearest wire cage, one of a dozen or so lining two walls of the room used for her furry patients. Sadie slipped on her gloves. Cara did the same with the pair she kept in her back pocket.

It'd be tricky, taking the lid off of this tub and easing the squirrel into the cage. She didn't fault the woman for putting her in the oversized container with one of those lids that didn't easily snap off. But it left too large of an opening for the squirrel to escape if she and Cara weren't careful.

"Ready?" Sadie slowly tilted the tub, listening to the squirrel try to gain its footing, its claws scratching at the slippery surface. She hoped to ease off the lid just enough that the squirrel might slip through and run right into the cage. It sure wasn't acting injured.

"Whenever you are," Cara answered.

She took a deep breath. "One, two...*three*."

The squirrel scrambled inside the box, not knowing what to make of the newest escape route. Even with gloves on, Sadie's finger suffered a nibble as the frightened squirrel paused where the tub met the cage's opening. The process took less than ten seconds, but Sadie still held her breath even after the squirrel hunkered down in one of the far corners of its cage.

"That wasn't so bad," Cara said, peeling off her gloves again.

"Tell that to my poor finger."

"I can match that and more," Cara said, slipping one arm out of her coat sleeve to push up the sleeve of her sweatshirt. An angry-looking red welt stretched wrist to elbow.

"Let me guess—Skeeter."

"The one and only."

That female raccoon had an ornery streak, but Sadie didn't blame her. She'd arrived with a nasty case of road rash. Her injuries had taken longer to heal only because she'd resisted treatment.

Cara rested her hands on her hips and looked around, squinting. Sadie guessed she'd lost her glasses again. For someone who needed them to see, Cara misplaced them on a regular basis. An inconvenience, she called them.

"What's next?" she said.

"Why don't you head to town now. We're desperately low on kibble. Brysons called to say the donation box is full again. Would you mind stopping by to pick up that, too?" Sadie tore a page from the small notebook she kept in the pocket of her shirt and handed it to her. "It's a small shopping list this time."

"On it," Cara said. She flipped up her hood again.

That's what she loved about Cara. Her new partner's willingness to do anything for the shelter with a smile was such a relief. Sadie had shouldered the responsibility for everything for the last two years, so having someone like Cara to share the burden—physically, financially, and emotionally—was huge. She loved the social media part, too, which Sadie hated. Now the shelter had an online presence which helped with outreach and donations.

"Oh, there's an opossum coming in some time today. I got a call from someone in Erie," Cara said, shaking her head. "They captured it in their live trap and the poor thing's foot was injured in the process."

Sadie rolled her eyes. Humans were the biggest problem when it came to injured wildlife.

Cara left as the first flakes of the season fell outside. They'd have to double down to get the outside enclosures cold-proofed. Sadie had heard it'd be an early winter.

She pinned a few shoulder-length stray hairs into the clip on the back of her head yet again, opened the cage that held two infant red fox squirrels, and scooped them both into her cupped hands. The cage across the room was cleaned with fresh bedding. The squirming babies almost made her lose control, so she hurried past the exam table in the middle of the room to get to the cage and under the heat lamp.

But as she passed the stationary island, a loose strip of metal trim which she'd planned to glue back in place for ages, hooked the back of her sweater, pulling her to a complete stop.

She twisted and pulled, but it held her fast.

*No good.*

Sadie peered underneath her raised arms until she could barely see the metal strip holding her captive. She groaned.

With her hands literally full, she couldn't release herself.

She retraced her steps, hoping it would release her, but that didn't work.

Pulling didn't help either. The sweater's fleece fabric was too thick to tear.

She could stretch and maneuver her body as much as she liked but the nearest cage was still several feet away.

The wall clock taunted her, ticking away the seconds when Cara would return in at least an hour. By that time, these little furry tornadoes would nibble their way through her gloves. Her only option: let them loose, undo the snag, and catch them again. The last part of the plan would be the challenge. With a million and one places in the room to hide, it would take all of the hour and possibly more to capture the babies again.

She looked down at her cupped hands, weighing this half-baked plan, if she could call it that.

*Oh, the life of a rehabber.*

It was times like this when sitting at her dining room table fielding customer calls for the utility company full-time sounded pretty...*uneventful*. At least the mundane job might add years to her life.

*If you can't find the humor in this, just quit now before you become more vested in this harebrained mission of yours.*

But didn't she literally love the unpredictability of rehabbing? Yes, she did. She could do without the round-the-clock feedings for the babies and being regularly bitten and scratched. This getting-hooked-on-the-equipment thing, well, this was a new one. She giggled, and an involuntary snort escaped, which made her chuckle even more.

"Help!"

The pointless plea was almost as ridiculous as the situation itself. With Cara on her way to Bedden, there was little to zero chance another person would stop by before Cara returned. Furever Friends Rehab Center was tucked into a wooded five acres, ten minutes from downtown Port Chance. If someone happened to pass the driveway off the highway, they'd never see the house, rehab building, or the newly renovated cabin which was now Cara' s home. Even when the trees lost their leaves completely, one had to purposely look to see any outline of a structure through the dense foliage.

She opened her cupped hands a smidgen, and two little faces peeked out.

"Okay, guys. This is how it's going to go down." This pep talk was as much for herself as it was for them. "I'm going to bend down as far as I can and release you. And when it's time for me to catch you, you're going to make it easy for me."

One of them nibbled on the exposed skin on her wrist as if saying, *Get on with it already!*

She squatted as far as she could and opened her hands. They

immediately bounded away from her to spots a few feet away and froze. It took them only a few seconds to realize they were free, and they scampered away in opposite directions.

Releasing herself from the countertop was a challenge. She couldn't quite get a hand on the snag to release herself. A cramp seized her side. She grimaced, fighting through the discomfort to reach her fleece.

Someone knocked on the door and immediately opened it with a blast of cold air.

"Shut the door!" she shouted.

The babies appeared for a micro-second before darting underneath the steel counter. One appeared at the far end before dashing toward a supply cabinet near the opened door.

An unfamiliar man stood frozen just inside the door, taking in the scene. And the door *still* wasn't closed.

"Close. The. *Door,*" she repeated again. A rude greeting, she knew, but she didn't care given her current predicament. "*Please.*"

To his credit, the stranger kicked the door closed behind him without asking questions. The force rattled the window.

"Looks like you're in a bit of a bind," he said with a touch of humor in his tone.

"I'm more worried about the two furry escape artists on the loose in here. Can you *not* tell me what I already know and just help me, please?"

"Where do you want th—?" He started to cross the room, but jumped and let out a yelp instead. "What was *that*?!"

Sadie half expected him to climb onto the nearest stool. Wide-eyed, he searched the floor. It was almost comical, watching a grown man—and a large, lumberjack-y one, too— become undone by a five-ounce fur ball.

"Baby squirrel. Hence my request to close the door." Sadie gestured to her sweater. "I'd like some help, please?"

He came closer. A flash of vulnerability at being pinned and finding herself at the mercy of a complete stranger made her heart race. It didn't help that he paused to study her again with that maddening half-grin.

"I'm Hayes, by the way," he offered finally as he pried the fabric from the splintered counter trim. He must have read her mind. "Hayes Kelley. Cara's brother."

The trim released its grasp on her sweater and she faced him, smoothing the garment around her hips. Relieved, she took a cleansing breath and finally tore her attention away from searching for the squirrels to look fully at Cara's brother.

A flush instantly warmed her face.

Hayes had the blackest hair she'd ever seen. A hawkish nose complimented the inky slashes of his full brows. There was a half-moon scar on his upper cheek. It was like the universe decided a face shouldn't be so symmetrical and added the tiny imperfection. In Sadie's opinion, it just made him more handsome.

"Thanks." She brushed herself off. Suddenly, she seemed to have too many hands and not enough poise to carry on a conversation. He looked vaguely familiar. "I'm Sadie...Wendell. You come...*came* at the rice...*right* time." She almost palmed her face at the blunder.

He wasn't fazed by her awkwardness. Instead, the missing squirrels preoccupied him.

"What exactly did I walk in on?" he asked as he squatted to look under the stainless counter against the wall.

"I was transferring two infant squirrels into a clean enclosure when I got caught. I had to let them loose to help myself.

8

As you can see, that didn't work out as planned." She planted her hands on her hips, scanning the room.

"And then I saved the day."

She looked at him sharply, caught off guard by his bold words.

"Sorry, that was kind of weird. Did Cara warn you about me?"

She really needed this guy to leave so she could find these squirrels. Across the room, a spindly tail disappeared behind the waste basket. On second thought, it was time for her to put him to the test.

"Nope." She pulled out a collapsible tunnel from where she kept enrichment toys for the animals. "But that doesn't matter. It's time for you to save the day again."

*Chapter Two*

S ave the day, she'd said. *She's mocking me.*

Hayes leaned against the center island while this woman scurried around him, keeping her eyes on the floor. She yanked a pink polypropylene bag from the corner of the room, gave it a shake, and tossed it to the floor as it transformed into a child's play tunnel. She worked silently and purposefully.

"Can I help?"

She stuck a finger in the air. "In a minute."

He crossed his arms while she unfolded three portable gates and positioned one on either side of one of the tunnel's openings. The third gate blocked the opening on the other end.

"You look like you know what you're doing, but I'm happy to do something."

The table he leaned against moved a hair, throwing him off balance. The wheels screeched across the concrete floor as he spun to catch himself from falling.

Sadie rummaged through a cabinet but turned around at

the commotion, narrowing her eyes. "Maybe just stay put for another minute," she said wryly.

He pulled the table back in place, toeing down the brake on the nearest wheel, and waited for directions. In the meantime, he wracked his brain trying to place where he'd seen this woman before. She looked so familiar.

His sister mentioned her new partner in passing a few times. Said she ran the most efficient wildlife rehab center Cara had seen. Not quite petite, Sadie was fine-boned nonetheless and carried herself with an air of quiet, no-nonsense competence. Her shoulder-length auburn hair recorded every movement as she cast furtive looks in his direction. Inquisitive eyes, defined by arcing brows, lent her a dubious look. He didn't blame her, barging into her shelter unannounced.

*Have I met her somewhere?*

"What brings you here?" Sadie asked a minute later as she rested one hand on the top of a broom handle while still scanning the floor for the two furry escapees. It was clear she wanted him to leave.

"Cara asked me to stop by to help her move a desk into the cabin."

She nodded, waving the broom next to the shelving unit against the wall, trying to flush them out.

"I sent her on an errand. She should be back in an hour or so," she said with another darting glance in his direction.

"I can just wait at her place—"

"At your feet! Watch OUT!" Sadie shouted, coming at him with the broom.

He instinctively ducked from the impending assault and whirled around, catching sight of one squirrel who zipped under the exam table. Should he hop onto the table to get out of the way, freeze, or run for the door? By the crazed look in Sadie's eye, it might be safest to leave.

"Get him!" Sadie dropped to her knees, peering under the table, then rebounded onto her feet with the ease of an extreme body shock instructor, darting to the other side of the table. Too late. The squirrel disappeared behind the supply cabinet again. She straightened, exertion coloring her cheeks. A strand of hair fell over her eyes before she impatiently pushed it out of the way. "You can help now, you know."

Hayes felt dazed. This woman's agility at getting onto the floor and upright again was remarkable. "You haven't explained the plan."

Sadie blew air from her cheeks while re-pinning strands of hair into the clip she wore at the back of her head. It was an ordinary action, but for some reason, captivating.

"I'm trying to herd them into...there." She pointed to the tunnel. "It's not ideal, but it's the best I've got at the moment." Mumbling about her lack of a net, Sadie's frowned deepened.

Now that he understood, they spent the next few minutes darting around the room, chasing the squirrels out from under their hiding places. He and Sadie came close to catching the little buggers several times, but the babies were skittish and nimble, a combination that proved successful at avoiding capture.

Hayes rested his forearms on the exam table, breathing hard. He was too big which meant he also wasn't very agile. Across from him, Sadie's brows still pinched together in frustration.

"Cara is better at this than I am. Maybe we should pause until she comes back." He hooked his thumb toward the door. "I can go do what I came for, move that desk."

Sadie shook her head before he even finished talking.

"You're not leaving this room until I catch those guys. You're lucky they didn't run out when you came in." She repositioned one of the gates near the tunnel, tripping in the process.

"Fair enough."

"Oh!" Sadie whisper-shouted. "Look!"

One of the squirrels rushed out into the open, toward the mouth of the tunnel. As he paused, the other one appeared a foot away. Sadie spread her arms wide and hunkered down, creeping toward them like a human glider. They dashed around in a frenzied circle, then disappeared inside the pink tunnel. Meanwhile, he tripped over his own foot, almost crashing head-on into the refrigerator.

"Got 'em!" she hooted as she slid one of the gates in front of the opening.

"Now what?" He steadied himself on the exam table again. Hayes thought he was in good shape after lifting at the gym four nights a week. He'd have to add squirrel chasing to his workout regime.

"One of us will lift that end so they slide into"—she lifted a cardboard box off the floor behind her—"this."

He stuck his hand up. "I volunteer as lifter."

"You may have a future in the rehab business after all," she said with a small grin.

Maybe she did have a sense of humor after all.

Transferring the babies back into their cage proved uneventful. Sadie locked them inside and turned to him. "I bet that was a first for you. You're officially certified in wildlife capture."

"Can't wait to tell the guys at work."

"I'm sure they'll be impressed."

He didn't want to leave, but couldn't think of a good

reason to stay. Sadie's attention was focused on her laptop now anyway. It was a good time to leave.

"I'm just going to wait for cabin at her Cara." He grimaced. *What a bumblehead*. "Strike that. I'll wait for Cara at her cabin." He'd apparently grown an extra limb or two and learned how to speak in strange tongues in the last twenty minutes.

Sadie nodded, biting her lip to hide a smile. "Thanks for the help."

As he left the shelter, he snuck a look through the front window as he passed by and caught Sadie laughing to herself as she scribbled something into a notebook. It was only a split second, but that's all it took for Hayes to form a solid opinion of Sadie Wendell.

And that opinion meant he'd be finding another excuse to show up at Furever Friends Rescue sooner rather than later.

# Chapter Three

L ater that day, Sadie pulled up a chair at the table, her dinner plate heaped with a slice of pork loin with cranberry chutney, a cloud of mashed potatoes with a river of gravy seeping over one side, and an obligatory helping of almond green beans. She wasn't a fan of green beans, but her mother always got after her and her sisters, even though they were all two decades into adulthood, give or take a few years.

It was elbow to elbow at the Wendells' long dining room table. Her oldest sister, Rose, and her husband, Jordan, and their three boys were the first to seat themselves. Second oldest, Janie, and her fiancé, Mark, carried two steaming bowls of mashed potatoes across the room from the kitchen. There was a frantic jostling of bowls and platters to make room for each new addition. At the kitchen counter, their mother, Sonya Wendell, covered the remaining meat with aluminum foil and joined the group at the table. Aaron Wendall appeared a minute later with his grill tools, which he dropped into the sink with a clatter.

Rose was the first to compliment Sonya Wendell on the meal.

"It's delicious, Mom. I don't think you've made this version before, have you?"

The front door banged open and a halfhearted groan floated into the dining room.

"Must be Calamity Kit," Sadie said under her breath, but half the table caught it. There was a collective snicker.

"Sorry we're late," Kit said as she surveyed the almost-full table while holding a bowl covered with plastic wrap. "Did Janie eat all the food yet?"

"Nope, plenty of food left for everyone," Janie said. She stood to take the bowl from Kit while she slipped off her coat. "I just ate your portion."

"The marina wasn't ready for the Dolly Swain this afternoon," Kit said in apology, pulling out a chair. Holden Berne, a friend from high school she'd recently reconnected with, settled next to her. "I had to wait around forever for them to take her out of the water."

"Be thankful they were able to do it today," their father said. "I heard more snow is on the way this week."

Sadie made a mental note to keep an eye on the forecast. She and Cara couldn't waste time prepping the outdoor enclosures if an extended weather system moved through the area.

The conversation moved from Kit's last tour group of the season, a birding-watching group, to twelve-year-old Travis's prospects for starting on the junior high basketball team. Mark brought up that he'd heard Tom Hicklebourne planned to have the newly rebuilt Yellow Pier Restaurant reopen in time for the New Year.

"He's really moved fast getting that finished, hasn't he?" their father said. "Just under two years."

"I told him if he finishes by March, it'll be our first choice for the rehearsal dinner," Janie said. "He knows how big our extended family is."

"Is it big *enough*?" Sonya asked.

Sadie listened to her family's banter while she ate. Her hunger reminded her that she'd skipped lunch because the day had gotten away from her. The morning started with a meeting at the utility company she worked for as a customer service rep. It'd run into overtime, causing her to reschedule a visit from the department of natural resources field officer who wanted to inspect her facility over the lunch hour.

"I heard you had a special visitor at the rescue today," Rose said, eyeing her.

Had Rose read her mind? She'd mentioned that awaiting the state inspection was stressful, but she didn't expect them to remember today was the day. "Yes, and what a relief. The field officer checked out the building and gave it an 'A' on his score-card. The only point of improvement—"

"Field officer? No, I'm talking about Cara's brother. What was his name—Jay, Ray...?"

"Hayes. His name is Hayes. He literally just showed up today," she said. "How did you hear about him?"

Rose cleared her throat. "He stopped at the bakery down-town to ask for directions. He went on and on about the slice of cherry sour cream coffee cake he picked up, too. I told him he earned 'favorite customer of the day' status for that. Nice guy." Rose looked pointedly at her at the last part. "Kit met him, too."

Kit's brows wiggled when Sadie glanced at her. "*Very* nice guy," Kit teased.

Rose had recently opened a bakery storefront in downtown Port Chance, an extension of the one at Apple Hill Farm. Her bakery manager, Linn Miranelli, made most of the pastries and donuts for both locations, but Rose's specialty was her cherry sour cream coffee cake. It was her signature recipe, which she liked to joke wasn't consistent with the business's apple theme, but why not embrace your talent, she reasoned.

Sadie sighed. Her big, talkative family spent way too much time fretting about her being alone "with just animals for company," her mother liked to say. That they knew the minute Hayes Kelley showed up in town annoyed her, but she'd grown used to it. Rarely did anything of importance fly under the Wendell clan's radar. They'd called Port Chance home for five generations. It was unusual in this day and age for a family to plant roots in the same hometown where they'd grown up, but that was the case for Sadie and her three sisters. Janie and Kit had escaped for a few years, taking odd jobs across the country, testing the pull of familial and hometown bonds, but they'd eventually found their way back to Port Chance.

"Will this Hayes person be sticking around for a while?" Sonya asked.

"I don't know. You'll have to asked Cara." Sadie kept her eyes on her plate lest she give her mother any fuel to fan the flames of speculation.

"We should invite him to dinner," Kit crowed.

"Seriously?" She put down her fork. "We don't even know him."

"It's Cara's brother, for Pete's sake," Sonya said. "It's not like he's a total stranger." Sadie caught the wink her mother shared with Kit.

*Fine*. If they wanted to play at her expense, let them. Her family had made it clear for years—nine years since her divorce to be exact—that it was time to move on from her disastrous marriage. And "move on" translated to "look for another husband" in Wendellspeak.

*No, thank you.*

She was perfectly contented with her life. She made her own schedule. She answered to herself, and no one else.

Janie caught her at the door an hour later as Sadie slipped her coat on to leave.

"Sorry for the chatter about that Hayes guy," Janie said. "You know they're just playing." Janie was the only one who didn't take part in their good-natured teasing. For some reason, her sometimes brash, outspoken older sister was sensitive to the topic of Sadie's nonexistent romantic life.

"I know they are. Sometimes it just gets old." She waved away Janie's concern. "I probably just left my sense of humor at home today."

Janie offered a solemn nod before her expression brightened. "Oh! I made an appointment to try on wedding dresses in Greenhaven. Will you come?" Janie asked.

"Of course. I wondered what you've been waiting for." Janie and Mark planned to be married in May at Apple Hill Farm. It was months away, but already Rose had ordered decorations for the dessert table and enlisted Jordan and the boys to build a cedar gazebo near the event barn. "I wouldn't miss it."

"I'll say something to Mom and Kit about laying low on the talk." Janie reached out for a quick hug. "You don't have to put on a show for me. I know it bothers you."

Sadie zipped her coat. "It really doesn't in the grand scheme of things. Mom in particular has never accepted the fact that I'm good by myself. I'm happier this way."

Janie hitched a brow at that.

She threw the most convincing grin she could muster at Janie. "Truly."

* * *

Cara's cabin was lit up like a Christmas tree when Sadie pulled into the driveway a short time later. A thin wisp of smoke from the wood stove pipe wafted skyward, backlit by a sliver of moon. The window sheers did little to obscure the view into the front room, which joined the eating area and kitchen behind it. Two dark forms sat opposite each other at the round dining table. Sadie slowly coasted by the window, hoping for a glimpse of what Cara and Hayes were up to inside.

A melancholy had settled in her chest as she left her parents' house earlier. Maybe it was the combined effect of Kit and her mother's teasing and the fact that each of her sisters had found love. Maybe it was because Christmas was on the way, her most favorite holiday, and she'd yet to regain her joyful anticipation for the month ever since her divorce.

Sadie slid out of the driver's seat and closed the door at the same time that the door to the cabin opened, flooding the small porch with light.

"Hey, Sadie! Hayes and I are playing cards. Want to join us?"

"No, thanks. I'm heading to bed. Long day." She waved as she headed down the sidewalk to her front door, cutting through the area between Cara's cabin and the intake building. There was a little stand of cedar in front of the house, and earlier that spring she'd planted a pollinator garden in between the buildings. It was now her favorite area of the property, a magical little path lit with solar lights hanging on miniature shepherds hooks. Someday she'd extend the driveway so it looped around to her house and she didn't have to park so far away. Maybe she'd add a garage, too. Truth be told, she liked that people didn't have easy access to her front door. But for now, the winding pathway was a sweet concession that greeted her at the end of the day.

"Are you sure? I just made popcorn. And I have drinks," Cara said.

"I'm good. I'd slay you both with my mad blackjack skills anyway. Your fun evening would go downhill fast." She planned to make a quick dinner, give her good friend Rory Hilt a call since they'd been playing phone tag for a few days, then hit the pillow early.

"That sounds like a challenge," Hayes shouted through the open door behind Cara.

"Not a challenge, just reality," she called. The man was friendly enough, but he left her feeling edgy. He was too handsome for his own good; that was part of it. Cara didn't need to witness how her brother affected Sadie either. She continued walking.

"If you change your mind…" Cara called.

Sadie gave Cara one last wave over her shoulder. "You two have a good night."

She kicked off her boots inside the door and wound her way through the house, switching on lights. Rummaging through her cupboards, she grabbed a new jar of salsa and hopped twice to reach the bag of tortilla chips on the top shelf. The bag came down on her head while she bruised her hip against the countertop.

While she bent over the kitchen sink to wait for the pain to subside, she looked out her window toward Cara's cabin. It gave her a different view of Cara and her brother seated at the dining room table. Something Hayes said made Cara throw back her head with a laugh. Hayes held his head in his hands with a dramatic show of frustration. That made Cara laugh even more.

She smiled despite the glumness gnawing a hole in her chest. Why the sight of a brother and sister enjoying each other's company made her feel that way was a mystery. But it stayed with her even as she turned out the lights that night and went to sleep.

# Chapter Four

Hayes had lost count of the number of blackjack hands they'd already played. The night started with five-card stud, but Cara grew bored with beating him. So far, he was holding his own with this game. His pile of popcorn grew exponentially with each win. Now he wanted to know more about his sister's new partner, the one she'd talked his ear off about earlier in the summer.

"What's she like, your partner?"

"Haven't I mentioned Sadie before?" Cara's voice trailed off as she studied her hand. "I thought I had."

"Not really." A little lie. He knew Sadie was thirty-something. Quiet. Divorced. And she loved animals. He didn't need anyone to tell him that.

"She's smart. Thorough. And *fast*. Literally. Did you know she finished the Fall Run Under the Sun this year with the shortest time ever recorded in the history of the event?" Cara's eyes bugged as she kept her attention focused on the cards.

"The fall what?"

"It's a little 5k up in Dubuque right along the river. Super pretty that time of year."

That would explain Sadie's crazy quick moves that he'd witnessed in the other building earlier that day. Her agility was astounding.

"And she grew up in the area, too, right?"

"Born and raised in Port Chance," she said, ticking up an eyebrow. "How many cards?"

"Two." He laid down his discards and picked up the two Cara dealt him. *Oh well.*

"You know, you two have something in common." Cara's attention darted to him then back to her cards as quick as a blink.

"What's that?"

"You're both hermits," Cara said as she dropped her cards on the table. Two fives and a king. Her luck at blackjack had turned.

"I'm nowhere near a hermit."

Cara shot him a skeptical look. "Every time I call you, you're at home watering your plants or tying flies or whatever."

He sat back in his chair. "First of all, I have one succulent that I've nursed along for six years now, ever since what's-her-name left."

"Ooo, she was a piece of work." Cara snapped her fingers. "What was her name?"

"Blaine," he said flatly.

"That was it. I wasn't a fan. Totally wrong for you."

"I know. You made that clear the first time you met her."

Cara shrugged. "Someone has to watch out for you. How nice of you, to adopt her plant."

"I didn't have a problem with the plant, only her." He

picked up the deck and shuffled. "As far as tying flies? I can't fish without them, and they're a fortune to buy."

She lifted one of his hands, making him drop most of the cards. She made a show of studying it front and back.

"I've never understood how you manage to tie those tiny things with these monster mitts."

"It's never been a problem. And it's quiet work. I need the downtime at night. Helps me sleep." He reorganized the cards, shuffled, and dealt them again. "Let's go back to poker."

"Point made. When's your last day at the plant?" Cara asked as she picked up her hand. She snorted as she studied her cards. "I can't imagine you have a worse hand than I do here."

He hesitated. The auto plant he'd worked at for more than a decade planned to move production over the border to Wisconsin. His unit was given a choice: either agree to a transfer to the Beloit facility or take the severance package. As a product engineer, Hayes decided to take his chances on finding work somewhere else. His disappointment in management made it an easy decision. But he'd yet to tell Cara about the shortened timeline.

"Hayes?"

"It was last week."

"*What*?" Cara dropped her hand. "I thought they'd told you sometime before Christmas? Wait, are you not making the move to Wisconsin?"

"No, I decided to leave."

"So now you need to look for a new job? Was that smart?" Her shoulders slumped like they carried the weight of the world. Last time he checked, he was out of a job, not Cara.

"I'll do okay. They boosted my severance package, essentially telling me they wanted me gone anyway. I guess I made too much money, so they're hoping to find someone else who can do more work for less. It was hard to pass up."

"What about your place?"

"I'll list it in the spring. I'm in no rush to move out. Winter is a terrible time to try selling anyway."

"Wow. Merry Christmas." She scooped up her cards again to study them.

Hayes snorted. "No kidding."

"But where will you look for a new job?"

He shrugged as he laid down one card. "I could go anywhere really. Ohio. Michigan. There's a plant or two in Iowa."

"I'd prefer Iowa," she said under her breath. "Not that I'm going to dictate where you land."

"Never stopped you before."

"I'm mellowing with age," she quipped as she tossed a card face down on the table for him. "Thirty-eight years going on eighty. Hey." Cara sat up. "Here's an idea. Stay here with me for a while. If there are job prospects in Iowa, this could be your home base while you look."

"I don't need to be physically here while I job hunt. Actually, I have a phone interview the day after tomorrow, and two more later next week."

She shook her head, dismissing his comment while she forged ahead.

"Sadie won't mind you staying here. The couch is a pull-out. This place is huge for a one-bedroom. I won't even complain when you leave your toiletries scattered around the sink." She looked at him over her cards. "Where would the job be that you're interviewing for tomorrow?"

"Michigan." He played his hand. Full house. "I can't live with you. We'd kill each other."

"It's just until Christmas. You can tolerate me until then. *Please?*" Cara spread her cards on the table in front of them. A pair of nines.

"I'll think about it."

"That's all I'm asking for now. Hey, you win." A slow grin spread across her face. "That's a sign, you know."

"What is?"

She pointed at his hand. "Full house. That means you're staying here."

Hayes sighed. His sister was a bulldog. Unrelenting. "So much for thinking about it."

They played until their conversation was punctuated by yawns. Hayes took the armload of bedding that Cara pulled from her linen closet and floated a sheet and blanket over the convertible couch. It creaked and whined when he lay down a short time later.

"I'll do permanent damage to my back if I stay on this thing longer than a few nights," he joked as soon as Cara peered around the corner at the racket. "Staying through December is looking pretty bleak."

"If you'll seriously consider staying, I'll spring for the plushest mattress on the market."

"I'm not that great of company, Cara. Why do you want me here so bad?"

"It's just nice to have you around." She shrugged with a small smile. "I miss you."

He couldn't argue with that. They hadn't been able to spend much time together over the last few years with him working nonstop and Cara out in San Francisco. He readjusted his body to fit more comfortably between the metal frame. He could feel every rod and spring underneath the thin mattress. No way could he spend more than a night or two on this thing. Not unless ending up in traction was on his bucket list. It wasn't, last time he checked.

"I miss you too," he countered. "It was nice when we both had less responsibilities and more time, wasn't it?" A heartfelt admission from Cara was rare.

"Yeah, like twenty years ago." She laughed while rummaging in the hall closet, then she tossed another bed pillow in his direction. "Can't say I'd like a repeat of those years. I kind of like my life now."

"Who's the real hermit, though? You're living in a cabin in the woods, socializing with animals." He admired her work with the rescues, and Cara knew it. Only he could get away with poking fun at her.

"They're easy to love. You should try it."

"I'll stick to doting on my one succulent."

Cara giggled. "Someday you'll make a fine husband to some undeserving woman."

"I can't see you approving anyone suitable."

She clutched a hand to her chest. "What? I'm way beyond judging your choices for female companionship."

"You literally just admitted that whomever I marry will be undeserving."

She tapped her chin with a finger. "I did say that, didn't I? I guess you do listen to what I have to say."

He pulled the blanket around his chin. "Like it's gospel."

Cara rolled her eyes as she grinned. "Good night, big brother."

Hayes listened to Cara's fading footsteps on the wood floor

as she headed to her bedroom down the hall. Her door clicked shut a few seconds later.

He lay there in the dark, turning Cara's words over in his mind, thinking about what attracted him to a woman. His criteria had certainly changed over the years. Whereas once the outgoing, assertive types had caught his attention, Hayes grew bored with their constant need to be "seen."

Blaine had been a perfect example. They'd met in his late twenties while he attended a work function in Chicago. She'd approached him in the hotel bar—of course—and they hit it off. They swapped weekends, traveling the ninety minutes between their homes, to see each other. His weekends there were far different than her visits to Rockford. She loved nothing more than dressing him up and taking him along to whatever club happened to be the "it" place to be amongst her friends.

At first, he found her fascinating. A publicist for the Chicago Rockets, she was always "on." Her energy and look-at-me personality drew him like a bee to pollen. But the noise, the crowds, the flurry of expensive drinks landing in front of them all night long had grown old fast. That relationship had been a turning point for him. He'd grown to enjoy his solitude, even seek it. The women he found most attractive now were far from the Blaines of the world.

If he ever found himself in a long-term relationship again, that is with Cara's approval—who was she kidding?—she'd be someone who cherished her independence, just like his sister. She'd be smart and easy-going, too. She'd enjoy a peaceful existence, just like him.

Who was *he* kidding? His ideal partner sounded like a fantasy.

# Chapter Five

Sadie's feet hit the cold wood floor a few mornings later and she frowned at the unpleasant sensation. Even the gray sky alluded to a dreary day ahead when she lifted her bedroom shades. But by the time she'd had a cup of coffee, fed the animals, and glanced over her emails, her frame of mind shifted, thanks to the first message in her inbox. It came from a family who'd shown up at the rescue last month with a furry patient. She smiled when their name appeared on the email header.

*Hi Sadie:*
*Our inquiry today is two-fold: first, we're hoping for a continued good report on our fox friend. Your wonderful care is a godsend to the animals that come into your facility. Joselyn, Nell and I are thankful we found you.*

The young man named Jed and his daughter Nell had brought in a young fox, ridden with fleas and an advanced case of mange. It'd been found curled up on top of some burlap sacks in the corner of their shed. It was so sickly, the animal didn't even protest when they wrapped it in a blanket and transported it to Sadie's front door. Not ideal, handling a wild animal without proper equipment and experience, but thankfully, humans and the fox had arrived safely without problems.

After initial treatment, medication took care of the flea problem within the hour. Infection showed at some of the bite sites, so Sadie started a round of antibiotics, too. Treating the mange was more time-consuming, but doable. She'd keep the animal, which the girl had named Flora, through the winter and release it in the spring. Jed had checked in with her weekly since that first day, and sent two sizable donations. Sadie loved this aspect of wildlife rehabbing. Connections with appreciative patrons, the animals she healed and released back into the wild. Happy endings kept her spirits up. She read on:

*Also, we're wondering if you'd be open to an idea Nell had that would benefit you and her? It would involve a little education presentation at her school, and a fundraiser, a giving tree for the shelter, if you will. Please let me know if you'd like to hear more. ~ J*

She'd love to talk further, she responded. In the meantime, she'd loop Cara into the conversation, hoping she'd contact this family for a follow-up post on the rescue's webpage. Cara's feel-good stories always stirred a lot of online feedback and sometimes donations. Since Cara had permanently joined the rescue, a few of her posts had even gone viral.

After making herself another cup of coffee, Sadie wandered out to the carriage house at the back of her property, determined to capitalize on her uplifted mood. She followed the gravel drive, listening to a cardinal's song somewhere above her head, as she wound her way toward the building. Cara's brother's truck was still parked in front of the cabin. This was his third day here. Had Cara mentioned how long he'd be visiting?

Bringing her Christmas decorations into the house needed to happen, like, yesterday. Her mother's rule of thumb was to always have the tree up and decorated by the first of November. Sadie had followed that religiously until the divorce. Since then, her tree and decorations never made it out of the carriage house. A few years ago she convinced herself enough was enough; she was finally ready to decorate. But then the news that Evan was remarrying and there was already a baby on the way wove its way through the town grapevine and that tamped down her resolve.

Inside the building, Sadie stood in the cold, dim confines, peering up to the rafters. Frost collected around the roofing nails so it looked like a blanket of white stars hung on the underside of the pitched ceiling. Against the far wall, a set of simple wood stairs led up to the portion that had been floored for storage. She made her way over to the stairs now, determined to bring down her Christmas decorations. A boxed artificial tree and a plastic tote of ornaments wasn't too much trouble to bring down the steep, narrow stairs, but she really should tell Cara where she was headed. No need to invite trouble if she happened to fall and no one knew where she was. She stopped, one foot on the first step, reasoning she'd only missed her self-imposed deadline by a few days.

*But today's the day.*

Determined to ditch the dismal mood that crept up around the holidays, Sadie nodded to herself. A Wendell holiday was something to behold. Her mother started transforming the house on Halloween, hence Sadie's hard deadline. From the hand-stitched heirloom stockings lovingly sewn by Sadie's grandmother, to the twelve-foot Douglas fir freshly cut from Bonne Terre's Tree Farm in rural Greenhaven, her family's Christmases would feel right at home on a Hallmark movie set.

But as her marriage to Evan, her high school boyfriend, dissolved, so did her plans to share the Wendell family traditions with her own children sometime in the future. Sadie literally tucked all of those ideals away. She'd hated that Evan had affected her like that, but the hurt and disappointment over-shadowed the joy of the season. She hadn't been able to shake it.

She sighed as she gazed up at the rafters. Here she was again, attempting to regain what Evan so easily took away. But this year it was time. This year would be different.

Her hands slid down the railings until they fell at her sides. She shifted her weight, stepping back from the staircase.

She'd enlist Cara for help so they could haul the two boxes into her house together.

Or maybe she'd wait until tomorrow.

# Chapter Six

Hayes pushed aside the red gingham curtain over the kitchen sink with the butter knife, careful to not draw attention to himself. A slim figure in a hooded navy parka trudged back down the gravel drive from the carriage house. Auburn hair whipped around her face like a flag at the mercy of the elements.

Sadie.

She hunched against the brisk wind, ducking her head as it pushed against her. She zigzagged from its force until the narrow gap between the intake building and their cabin shielded her from the wind's force. Seconds later, she disappeared from view. He dropped the curtain back in place and spread raspberry jam on a piece of toast.

Hayes hoped to see her soon after the other night when Cara invited her to join their card party. She'd wasted no time turning his sister down, and since then had kept a low profile. Sadie might be more of a recluse than him.

Across the room, his phone rang.

Hayes dropped the knife in the sink, wiped his hand on a paper towel, and retrieved his phone from the coffee table.

He didn't recognize the number. The human resources person he'd interviewed with the day before for the Michigan job mentioned she'd lined up candidates to talk with all week. Today was way too early to learn if he'd made the cut, so it was most likely a spam call.

A knock on the door.

He silenced the phone before he opened the door.

Surprised, Sadie stepped back when he greeted her and almost lost her footing on the uneven steps.

"Oh, I thought—" She peered into the cabin behind him.

"That I was long gone? Cara convinced me to stay awhile longer." Sadie surely thought he was overstaying his welcome. "She borrowed my truck this morning."

"When will she be back?" She tried to look past him into the house. Twin circles of pink dotted each cheek from the cold. Sadie pulled her coat collar tight around her neck.

"After lunch." He stepped aside. "Do you want to come in? It's getting nasty out there."

Sadie took another step back, this time checking her footing.

"I'm fine." She hugged herself and visibly shivered. "Can you tell her I stopped by?"

"You bet. Are you sure?" He hooked his thumb over his shoulder. "I can brew us a quick cup of coffee."

"Thanks, but no." Sadie paused for a split second like she might change her mind, but then the corner of her mouth turned down. "I have a lot to catch up on."

"If you change your mind..."

She smiled and gave him a halfhearted wave. "See you later."

Hayes closed the door, disappointed. Catching Sadie Wendell's attention was like trying to harness a hummingbird. *Impossible*. He might need a cup of coffee himself to offset the chilly vibe she'd given him.

He plucked his phone off the table, noting the voicemail notification. As he scooped grounds into a fresh filter, he listened to the message.

*Hayes, it's Brett Huber from TriTech Logistics.*

The Michigan job. He held his breath.

*Thank you for interviewing with us the other day. It was great talking with you. Just wanted to touch base about the search.*

Judging by this guy's tone, it wasn't good news.

*While your credentials were beyond impressive, we've found someone who's a slightly better fit.*

He ended the voicemail with a finger tap before the man finished speaking and tossed his phone onto the couch.

*Ah well*. It was for the best. Cara dreaded him working so far away, too. He wasn't fond of the idea either, but a job was a job. Now that Michigan was officially off the table, he *was* a little relieved.

Cara burst into the cabin at that moment in her typical flurry of shuffled bags, thumps, and heavy sighing. She'd perfected the art of announcing her arrival without saying a word.

"The roads are icing over. I hope you don't have plans to go anywhere," she said as she slung a shopping bag onto the kitchen island. "A Jeep literally did a three-sixty two cars ahead of me. I decided to get back here sooner than I wanted."

"Good thinking." He leaned back against the counter and tucked his hands in his pockets. "Nope, I'm in for the day. Hey, you'll like to hear this."

She stopped unpacking groceries, a can of tuna poised in mid-air. "Job news? Please don't tell me you're moving."

"You're not going to get rid of me any time soon."

Cara pumped her fist. "Yes!"

"But I'm still on the lookout, and I need leads. If you know of any places hiring a mid-level powertrain engineer." He pointed at himself.

She gritted her teeth and resumed unloading groceries. "What does that even mean? In layman's terms, please."

"It's basically everything that delivers power to make a vehicle move."

"Simple enough. I'll ask around." She winked. Sarcasm was Cara's second language.

"Sadie stopped by looking for you."

Cara tossed a small bag his way. "Oh, yeah? What'd she want?"

Honey roasted peanuts, his weakness.

"She didn't say. Just wanted you to give her a call when you got home."

Cara nodded. "Noted."

"Maybe you should call her now."

"I will after I finish putting groceries away."

"It could be an emergency."

Cara paused again with an exasperated sigh. "Did she look like she was in distress?"

"I mean, maybe?" She'd looked cold, but that wasn't a medical emergency.

She chuckled. "So you're not certain? How about *you* give her a call since you're so concerned." Cara toyed with him again, judging by the twinkle in her eye.

He ripped the top from the peanut bag and shuffled a

handful into his mouth so she wouldn't see his lips twitch. His lips always twitched when she put him on the spot, and she liked poking fun at his obvious sign of discomfort.

"She specifically asked for you," he said. "I offered her coffee, but it was a no-go."

"Yeah, Sadie doesn't drink coffee after noon. Gives her heart palpitations." She tossed him a second bag of peanuts. "For tonight. After you finish the first one."

"You're going to buy me pants with a bigger waistline next, right?"

# Chapter Seven

The early snow storm warning had popped up on Sadie's weather app the night before, and now almost a week after the baby squirrels incident, Sadie finally transported supplies from the shed into the intake building in preparation for bad weather. Alongside Cara, they filled the ATV with bags of bedding and food for the next few days. Then they drove the short distance across the property to unload.

Sadie hopped out of the vehicle to open the back lift gate. They hunkered into their coats against the wind as they carried the first load inside.

"I have a favor to ask." She took bags of kibble from Cara's arms and emptied them one by one into one of the plastic bins. "I got an email the other day from Jed Killeen."

"Flora's Jed? Let me guess. They wanted another update on their fox friend," Cara said as she stuffed the empty bags into the trash.

"That and they asked if we'd do a presentation for Nell's school."

A knowing smile spread across Cara's face. "Your worst nightmare—public speaking."

"Right. So I told him I'd check with you." Cara loved taking on the outreach programs; she blossomed in front of a crowd. It was one of the main reasons for adding her as a partner.

"I'm all in! I mean, I've only done a handful of school events, but what a great outreach opportunity." She looked around the room. "Who will we take to be our furry ambassador?"

"I'd bring Mobley. He's calm enough for that large of a group."

She stuffed a bag of bedding onto the shelf underneath the examination table as she gave Mobley a sideways glance. The opossum busied himself with an avocado wedge in his cage, devouring it in noisy haste. She'd cared for Mobley since she'd found him last year as a baby. He'd most likely fallen off his mother's back and suffered neurological damage somehow before Sadie came upon him near the carriage house. He was mostly fine except for a perpetual head tilt.

"They also want to do a fundraiser for us," she added.

"This just keeps getting better," said Cara as she replaced the trash lid.

"I know. Can I give you his contact info? Then you could take over logistics from here?"

"I'd be happy to." Cara shifted her weight onto her other foot while she chewed on her bottom lip. "Sadie?"

Sadie straightened with a hand on her back. A cramp in her side seized her breath and she rubbed the spot, hoping it was just a consequence of lifting the bulky bales.

"What's up?"

"Would it be okay if Hayes sticks around a while longer?"

She stopped rubbing her back. Their first awkward encounter popped into her mind. Being in close proximity to him, just the two of them, threw her for a loop. Her hand instinctively went to her neck as she remembered how her skin grew hot under his gaze.

"If it's not, no big deal," Cara said in a rush. "I mean, he's between jobs at the moment, and he could land another at any time—"

"He looks like he's already settled in."

Cara's mouth froze in a little "o."

"When I stopped by yesterday, his suitcase looked like it exploded. There was a new chest of drawers in the living room." She added with a grin. "It wasn't hard to put two and two together."

"Now I'm embarrassed. I'm so sorry. I should have spoken up sooner." She tapped her forehead with her palm. "It's just that he's having a rough go of it, you know, he's a bit of a workaholic."

This surprised her. Hayes didn't seem as tightly wound as she expected of someone who lived and breathed his job. In fact, she found his laidback demeanor attractive.

"And it's quieter here than if he stayed at our parents' place," Cara continued.

"It's fine. But you're sure the cabin is big enough for two people? I mean, you could always use my spare bedroom if this is a temporary thing."

"No, I can't impose like that. We'll be fine."

"What does he do, exactly?" It was a question that came to mind early on, but she hadn't found the right time to ask.

"He's an engineer. For cars. Don't ask for any more than that. He's tried to explain it to me, but it doesn't stick." She laughed. "But his company forced him out. Cutting costs and all that baloney. Meanwhile, top-level management continues to get the six-figure bonuses." She rolled her eyes.

"Of course." She lead Cara outside again to grab the last load.

"I mean, Hayes isn't hurting for money, that's for sure. He's an *engineer*, for goodness sake. But I keep telling him he needs to bump his boss out from behind that big, fat mahogany desk and take *his* job."

Sadie laughed. "But that's like someone telling us we should be veterinarians instead of rehabbers. Maybe he's doing exactly what he wants to do."

Cara planted her hands on her hips and gave her an incredulous look. "You know, now that you put it like that, that's absolutely right. You're brilliant."

"That's only because I've wondered why I didn't go to vet school maybe a million times, especially when it comes time to pay the bills around here," she said, handing Cara two bags. "But it always comes back to this: I'm passionate about what I do."

"Same. I couldn't walk away from this *ever*."

Sadie paused. "Where is Hayes anyway? We could have used him to lug some of this stuff, too."

"I think he said he had another phone interview. He mentioned stopping at our parents' house for something."

The one time she'd have welcomed seeing Hayes around here he'd found something else to do.

Sadie slipped the last bag of bedding from the back of the vehicle, tucking it under her arm and gingerly walked on the slick walkway. Ahead, Cara scuffed along the sidewalk, careful to avoid the uneven surface of the pavers while hugging the bags close to her chest. Sadie really needed to redo the sidewalk. They'd heaved over the last winter, and she'd meant to redo them when the ground thawed, but the summer and fall got away from her. *Next spring*, she vowed to herself.

"Let me get the door for you," Sadie shouted above the wind.

Cara turned slightly, nodding over her shoulder. She was upright one moment, and in the next, she lost her footing and dropped the bags she carried, landing on her side.

"Cara!"

Her partner lay perfectly still for a moment, and Sadie feared she'd hit her head. But then Cara sat up, her knit hat askew, and looked around. Sadie rushed the few steps ahead to check on her.

"Are you okay?"

Cara rubbed her thighs. "I think so? This marshmallow of a coat saved my back, that's for sure. But my elbow...I think it took the brunt of the fall." Her voice was strained, but other than that, her pain level was hard to read by all outward appearances.

Sadie dropped her bag and helped Cara to her feet. Cara winced when she stood.

"I think it's just a little ankle twist. I'm good." Except she couldn't put weight on it, reaching for Sadie to balance on one foot.

"Nonsense. Stay off of it for a while. It may be worse than you think." Sadie hooked her arm around Cara's back to help her into the building, avoiding her elbow just in case that was injured too. When Cara brushed her arm against the doorframe as they maneuvered over the threshold, Cara cried out.

"Your arm?" Sadie let go of her grip now that Cara was upright and inside.

"It's worse than I thought," Cara said through clenched teeth as she collapsed onto a stool inside. "Help me get this coat off."

It was a process. Sadie slipped the coat from her good arm and around her back, but removing the sleeve from the injured arm was not easy. Cara grimaced and moaned as Sadie inched the fabric off her arm. Her complexion looked ashen and moist by the time Sadie let gravity take over as the coat fell away from her hand.

"You need to see a doctor." She wasn't about to help Cara out of the fleece top after what she'd been through with the coat. "Where does it hurt exactly?"

Cara pointed to her elbow. "I can't even extend it."

"And your ankle?"

Cara gritted her teeth. "Not good, but my elbow's worse."

"Should I call Hayes?"

"No," she said with a humorless laugh. "He's not very good in a crisis."

Sadie didn't ask what that meant, but he'd need to know eventually. Instead of trying to convince Cara to call her brother, she draped the coat over her shoulders again, pulled Cara's hat over her head, and took the truck keys from her own pocket.

"Let's get you to the ER."

"What about the outside shelters?" Cara's complexion now matched her pale coat. She eased herself from the stool so Sadie could help her hobble outside.

"I'll take care of them later."

## Chapter Eight

Hayes wheeled into an empty parking space outside the hospital, sliding the last few feet on the icy pavement. He hurried toward the entrance as fast as the treacherous pavement allowed him. The snow was really coming down now. Fat snowflakes caught on his eyelashes as he blinked them away and melted on the exposed skin at his neck.

He'd finished with another phone interview seconds before Sadie's call came through. Her voice was off even as she assured him everything was all right. Cara had taken a fall. She was getting X-rays now.

Inside, the attendant at the check-in window led him through the double doors into one of the curtained rooms. Sadie sat alone in the room. Her hair, wet with snow melt, hung around her shoulders. The glum expression she wore didn't take away from her fresh-faced beauty.

*Don't forget why you're here. Focus on your sister.*

"Any news?" He sat beside her, second-guessing himself as he scooted his chair away to put a little space between them. She glanced his way with a thin smile.

"Not yet. They took her back about fifteen minutes ago."

He nodded. "What happened?"

Sadie sighed while she fidgeted with her hands in her lap.

"We were carrying supplies into the building. It'd already begun to snow and the sidewalk was slick. She lost her balance and went down hard." A frown creased the skin between her brows. "She didn't want me to call you. As far as she knows, I didn't."

"That sounds like Cara. She always thinks she's bothering me." Sadie's hazel eyes had brightened under the fluorescent lights. He looked down at his own hands to keep from staring. "I'll play dumb, say I tracked her or something."

Sadie stood to slip off her coat. He caught a wave of floral notes amongst the otherwise sterile smells of the hospital. She looked down at him as she draped the coat over the back of her chair. "She said you don't do well in situations like these either."

He laughed. "I'll give her that, but she tends to take things less seriously than I do."

"Is that another way of saying you overreact?" Sadie grinned as she sat again.

"Maybe. She's also the clumsiest person I know. This isn't her first ER rodeo by any means."

Her laughter reminded him of wind chimes, light and musical. "Then your vast experience with an accident-prone sister should calm your fears."

"If anyone can come through an adverse situation, it's my sister. Tough, like leather. She doesn't shy away from trouble, but doesn't intentionally look for it either. Her ex-husband was a piece of work, and now he's history." Knowing that Sadie's own marriage had ended disastrously, he regretted the last comment. That was the trouble with sitting in a quiet room alone with Sadie. In the short time he'd known her, he felt comfortable around her. Comfortable enough that his normally intact filter had failed, prompting him to overshare. In his peripheral vision, Sadie sat as still as stone. He hoped that wasn't a sign that his comment about Cara's marriage made her uncomfortable.

The curtain drew back as a nurse pushed Cara into the room in a wheelchair.

"The doctor will be in at some point to go over the X-rays with you," the woman said.

He waited for the nurse to leave. Cara was already frowning at him.

"What?" she said.

"How's the arm?"

"Hurts," Cara said flatly. "You didn't have to come. They'll probably prescribe some pain meds and I'll be good to go."

Her tone was curt. Cara still sounded sore at him for not jumping at the chance to stay in town with her through the holidays.

"Did they X-ray your ankle too?" Sadie asked.

Cara lifted it slightly to pull up her pant leg. "Yes, but it's hardly swollen at all. Just a little sprain."

"If you say so, Dr. Ortega," Sadie said under her breath with a little grin. "Looks bruised to me. That's not a good sign."

Coming from Sadie, the comment didn't draw the usual comeback from his sister. In fact, Cara clamped her mouth shut, shot him a sidelong glance, and folded her arms. Meanwhile, Sadie was the picture of calm.

They sat in silence for a while, the three of them studying the floor. Cara couldn't stay quiet for long. "Listen, I'm not being stubborn. I just don't think it's as bad as you both think.

Sure it hurts. I'll rest it for a few days. Hayes can stick around and help at the shelter—"

Sadie practically jumped out of her chair. "That's really not necessary. I can handle it."

Cara shook her head in protest. "This is all my fault for being clumsy. He'll be around anyway."

Sadie settled back against her chair as her attention bounced between them like she waited for the punchline. Now Cara had overstepped, making it look like they'd conspired behind Sadie's back, taking advantage of her hospitality before she'd barely gotten used to his presence.

He leaned forward to look at Sadie squarely. "That's not true. It's just wishful thinking on her part. I fully intended to leave to—"

Cara huffed good-naturedly. "You've made up your mind already? I thought you'd at least think about it."

"If you didn't jump to conclusions so quickly, maybe I could finish." Beside him, Sadie had clamped down on her lips so tightly, they'd turned white. He was cornered.

Cara let her head fall back against the wall. She let out an exasperated sigh. "I want to go home."

After a few seconds of silence, Sadie nodded decisively. "I think that's a good idea, you staying with Cara in the cabin. She'll need a hand getting around. We've already talked about it anyway."

Cara gaped at her. "You don't mind that he'll be sticking around for *weeks*?" She gestured toward him with her good arm. "See? I told you she'd be cool with it."

Now he *really* felt cornered. Sadie's poker face was first class except for the slight widening of her eyes when Cara mentioned "weeks."

"Whenever he's silent, it means he knows I'm right." Cara winked at him but directed her comment at Sadie.

"But I don't need help in the shelter," said Sadie. "Winter is the slowest time of year. I handled it by myself before you came along."

At that moment, the curtain opened and a woman regarded the three of them with an apologetic expression and a head shake. This didn't look good.

"Are you Cara's brother? I'm Dr. Hebren," she said, extending her hand toward him.

Cara sat forward in her wheelchair. "So, I'm ready to go home?"

The doctor looked over the tops of her glasses at Cara.

"Sure. As soon as we get you wrapped up."

Cara threw a smug look at him and Sadie. "See? Just a little bruised. I'll be good as new in a few days."

Dr. Hebren made a little grumble in her throat. "It's not that simple. Your elbow is fine. You'll definitely feel it for the next week or so, but there's nothing structurally wrong." She paused to glance at Cara's foot. "Your ankle, on the other hand, didn't fare as well."

"How so?" Cara said in a tone that had lost a little of its bluster.

"It's fractured. You'll need to meet with an orthopedic physician as soon as possible."

Hayes leaned forward. "And what does that mean, exactly?"

"We can wrap it up in a temporary cast today, but she'll need to see a specialist as soon as someone can get her in."

"I *broke* my ankle?" Cara looked up at the ceiling and groaned. "I don't have time for this."

"The good news is it looks like a clean break," Dr. Hebren

continued. "Eight weeks in a walking cast, crutches for the initial few weeks, is my guess. But the orthopedist will be able to give you a more definitive answer."

Sadie took Cara's hand.

"We'll get through this. It'll be fine," she said under her breath. Sadie glanced at him and gave him a slight nod as if reassuring him, too.

*Welp. This is my sign.* A cosmic smack on his head couldn't have been more obvious.

He'd be calling Port Chance home until Christmas after all.

# Chapter Nine

Sadie expected Cara had fractured her arm. What she didn't anticipate was Cara needing to stay off her feet for weeks. Now she really sank into a pool of guilt. Chances were the situation would've turned out differently had the walkway been fixed, and Sadie excelled at the "what if" game.

She and Hayes helped Cara back into the cabin a couple hours later. It was a literal scramble to shift furniture, removing obstacles so Cara could make it around the crowded space with her temporary cast and crutches.

"Maybe you two should move into my house and I'll take the cabin," she offered again after she and Hayes rolled up the rugs, moved end tables, and repositioned a recliner to make way for Cara as she struggled with the crutches. "With more room, you'd be less cramped for space."

"I've already said that I'm not displacing you from your own home," Cara said. She propped her crutches against the end of the couch as she sank into the cushions with a loud sigh.

"Besides, the less space I have to move around, the better. Crutching is exhausting."

A visual of Hayes sitting in her living room, bare feet propped up on her coffee table while watching television, flashed into her mind. An ordinary scenario, but it prickled the hairs at the back of her neck for some reason.

"Sadie?"

She jumped. Hayes and Cara looked up at her from where they sat together on the couch. Cara nudged Hayes with her elbow.

"See, I told you she's out of it. She's probably blaming herself for what happened to me," she whispered loudly enough that Sadie heard.

"Sorry. Long day." She rubbed the back of her neck. Her bed sounded pretty good right now. "And you're right. It's all my fault."

Cara waved the idea away. "That's silly. Hayes is making us dinner, and you're staying."

Sadie shook her head even before Cara finished talking.

"I have so much to catch up on. Maybe some other time."

"You'll miss out on the best lasagna you'll taste in your life," Cara shot back, nodding at Hayes. Hayes stared into his lap, smiling.

"Really, I can't." They'd spent three hours at the hospital. Now that it was almost dark, she'd have to wear her headlamp to hang tarps on the outside pens.

Cara tapped her chin with a finger. "I guess I'm too busy to do that school presentation for the Killeens, then."

Sadie gasped. "You're wicked."

Nodding, Cara eyed Hayes. "You'd agree, right?"

Hayes looked up at Sadie, his smile a little wider. There was a measurable look of delight on his face.

"Cara's negotiation tactics are fierce," he confirmed. "At least she's no longer twisting arms."

Cara let out a barking laugh. "Literally. You always gave in so easily," she said, throwing an arm around his shoulders. "He was twice my size but had half the fight."

He shrugged. "What can I say? I'm a lover, not a fighter," he said with a slight catch in his voice.

When Hayes met her eyes again, an electric pulse skittered through Sadie's every nerve.

"Then I guess I'm staying," she said.

Hayes turned out to be quite the cook. He'd whipped up a pasta sauce that Sadie swore was more fabulous than the food she'd sampled at Labriola's in Chicago two winters ago while on a shopping trip with her sisters. Every bite of lasagna melted on her tongue. She wasn't much of a salad fan, but she actually took seconds of the spinach, strawberry, and gorgonzola concoction he set in front of her with a sly grin after Cara crowed Sadie wouldn't touch it.

Their conversation wasn't as awkward as she anticipated either. Hayes cleared up the mystery surrounding what an automotive engineer actually does, and then admitted his latest interview had fallen flat, too.

"Something will come along, I'm sure of it," Cara said as she dabbed her mouth with a red gingham napkin.

"Are you looking to stay in the area?" Sadie asked before she cringed inwardly. The question sounded *hopeful*. It didn't make a difference to her whether he found a job locally or not, but Cara liked having her big brother close by. She'd cross her fingers for Cara's sake.

Hayes leaned back against his chair. "I'm open, I guess. The market isn't saturated with openings, so I'll count myself lucky if I find something in the area." He cast a quick glance at Cara who'd begun to stack their empty dishes on the table.

"Any more leads?" Sadie asked, this time keeping her tone in check, especially with Cara present. The woman had bionic ears and an overactive imagination.

"A recruiter contacted me the other day. We've set up an interview," he said, stealing looks at her while he talked.

"I hope it works out." *There. That didn't sound too awkward.* Cara shouldn't read too much into those words. She'd hobbled over to the sink.

"I'm not too worried. I have a little cushion with the severance package." He paused, then said louder, "I guess if my clumsy sister had to break her ankle, now was the time to do it."

Her back still turned, Cara gave them a little shimmy. Of course, she was listening.

"You're welcome to stay as long as you'd like," she said, lowering her voice. "The cabin is Cara's home. You don't need my permission to stay."

"I appreciate that. If you need help around here, I'd be happy to earn my keep."

Cara whirled around. "You didn't take care of the outside enclosures after we got back, did you?"

"Not yet. I can do them in the morning." From her peripheral vision, she noticed Hayes lean forward.

"I can help," he offered. "We'll get Cara settled on the couch, and we can head outside."

Her pulse hammered in her throat. Sharing a meal with him and his sister was one thing, but working alongside him alone was a different, more compromising scenario. It'd be dark. It was a two-person job, requiring four hands in close proximity. Better to wait until daylight. The foxes had access to their inside pens anyway. They were made for this weather, after all.

"Really, it can wait. It'll be an easier task in the morning. The wind is supposed to die down anyway."

"The wind is blowing from the north. You've even said the furnace can't keep up when the temperatures hit a certain point," Cara reasoned. "The tarps will help block the cold air from hitting that outside wall."

This was probably the only time in their relationship when Sadie didn't appreciate her partner's logic. Two against one. She didn't stand a chance of winning the argument this time.

"You'll need gloves and a hat," she said in a weak, last-ditch effort.

Hayes nodded. "In the car."

She chanced a look at Cara who was already crutching in the direction of the couch, no doubt trying to hurry along the situation. Cara beamed at her.

Sadie sighed. "Give me five minutes."

## Chapter Ten

Hayes knew what his sister was up to, but Cara playing matchmaker for her rescue partner and him wasn't the best idea. He'd have a little chat with her later, but now he wasted no time zipping his coat, then retrieving his hat and gloves from the truck's front seat.

Sadie met him outside a moment later, bundled in her calf-length parka. Her face was somewhere beneath her hood, and underneath that, a face mask. No amount of wind, snow, or ice pellets would penetrate her winter armor, that's for sure.

"Tarps are already in the intake building," she said above the howling wind.

"Lead the way," he shouted back. A gust pushed against his back. He squared his shoulders, bracing himself for more.

Freshly fallen snow added a couple more inches since they'd arrived home from the hospital. The knee-high drifts collected around tree trunks and his truck's front tires. Snow crunched under his hiking boots before they stopped in front of the intake building door while Sadie unlocked it.

Inside, animals stirred in their cages as soon as Sadie flipped on the lights.

"Hey, guys. Sorry to disturb your sleep," Sadie said in a soft voice.

She made the rounds in the room, stopping in front of each cage, murmuring in hushed tones. She paused longer in front of some of the animals. He stood silently while she did this, feeling like he intruded on some personal and reverent ritual.

"Okay," she said finally, facing him after a minute, her voice taking on a no-nonsense tone. "Let's get this finished so we can get back inside."

She pulled the lid off a large plastic garbage bin in the corner of the room and loaded his arms with folded tarps. After grabbing a box of bungee cords, Sadie led him out the back door nearest the outdoor pens.

Ice pellets nipped Hayes's cheeks as soon as he walked out from under the eaves. Cold fingers crawled down his parka, prickling his skin even under the layers. He and Sadie worked silently while taking turns unfolding the tarps and securing them to the chain-link enclosures with the cords.

Sadie accidentally elbowed him as she reached over their heads.

"Sorry. Close quarters." She smiled down at him as the lamp post that lit the area caught the glint in her eyes.

"I've experienced worse things on the job than an elbow to the head." A surge of warmth already rushed through him. Her hip pressed firmly against his while they stood side by side. Thank goodness this was silent work because he didn't trust his voice at the moment.

"Remind me to ask you for details once we're back inside," she said, raising her voice to match the storm's bluster.

Surprisingly, they worked efficiently even though the wind tried its hardest to work against them, wrapping the cumbersome tarps around their legs with each gust. When they hung the last tarp, Sadie scooped up the box of cords and scurried back into the intake building.

"I wasn't expecting this kind of weather so soon," Sadie said as she shut the door. She winced when she pulled off her gloves and blew into her cupped hands. "Can't even feel my fingers now."

He looked around the room. "What else needs to be done in here?"

She scanned the area, shaking her head. "I think we're good. Thanks for your help."

"My pleasure."

*Is she dismissing me*? He didn't want to leave just yet. That shield she so carefully hid behind hadn't come close to revealing the real Sadie Wendell. Would he be in Port Chance long enough to see that happen?

She snapped her fingers. "Actually, there is one more thing."

"Yeah?"

"Tell me about your worst experience." Sadie turned to fully face him now, leaning against the counter. Her all-business demeanor melted away as an eagerness transformed her expression. "I'm all ears."

He grinned. She hadn't forgotten.

"Last year, I stayed at work later than anyone else on my team."

"Where was this?"

"At the auto plant in Belemore. The floor where I worked was all windows." He leaned forward, propping his elbows on the examination table. "It was late January, so it was pitch-dark

63

outside at six o'clock. I only remembered what time it was because my watch's alarm buzzed then like it does every night."

"Why do you set the alarm to six o' clock every day?" she asked.

"I don't like to be there later than that, but sometimes I get into a zone."

She rolled her eyes. "I get that."

"Anyway, I'm sitting at my desk when the floor started rumbling."

"Like an earthquake?"

"That was my first thought. But then a fireball went up outside the window."

Sadie's eyes bugged. She pressed a hand against her chest. "Oh my."

"I couldn't see where it came from, so I ran to the windows on the other side of the floor."

"That sounds absolutely terrifying. I don't think I would've been able to move." She leaned forward too, folding her arms and resting them on the countertop.

"I froze initially, but then the alarms started going off so I high-tailed it to the stairwell." The sick feeling that he didn't have a second to spare still gripped his gut when the memories came back.

"Hopefully, it was only a few flights down?" she said.

"Four, but there were other explosions while I was heading downstairs. The lights went off. It sounded worse than when I was at my desk. Probably because of the echo chamber in the stairwell." Sadie's attention was glued to him now.

"So what caused it?" she asked. Her stiff posture and serious expression reminded him of Cara when she'd first learned of the accident. Cara had almost suffocated him with a hug.

"Several air compressors blew. Something malfunctioned nearby, causing them to overheat."

"Did anyone get hurt?" she asked in a whisper.

"A few guys. Only injuries, thankfully." He straightened. "That's when I got this little beauty." He pointed to the scar on his cheek.

"How?"

"Ran into the fire extinguisher on my way down the stairs."

"Ouch."

"But the worst part was we were overdue to replace some of the machinery that was affected—I was part of the redesign team for the upgrade—and we had to shut down that line. It hadn't been replaced by the time of the layoffs."

"And you were one of the layoffs?"

He nodded.

"I'm so sorry."

He shrugged. "Stuff happens for a reason."

The intense focus on his every word broke away. Sadie rubbed her hands together and looked around.

"That it does," she said distractedly as her brow furrowed for a split second. Then her face brightened again. "Anyway, I'm going to call it a night in here. Let's head out."

The wind seemed to pick up again as soon as they stepped outside like it'd been waiting to pummel them with its ferocity. Sadie locked the door again. He followed her across the pavers leading to Cara's cabin, but she turned left where the sidewalk veered off to a narrower walkway between the two buildings. She paused enough to give him a discreet smile over her shoulder.

"Thanks again for the hand," she said wistfully despite the smile. He'd barely had a chance to respond before she disappeared into the shadows of the white pine boughs hanging over her head.

## Chapter Eleven

Two mornings later, the woman on the other end of the phone was frantic. Sadie struggled to understand her at first amid the background noise: a radio station not quite in tune and something beeping—an unbuckled seatbelt, maybe? Doors slammed too—one, two, three—in heart-stopping succession.

"I'm on Route fifty-four outside of town. There's a groundhog, I think," the woman said a little too loudly into the phone with a tremor in her voice. "It's injured."

No matter how many calls like this Sadie fielded, they always jumpstarted her pulse. The thought of a suffering animal who wasn't yet in her care prompted a tug in her gut, too.

Sadie prepped the exam table and set out the necessary pain meds and the anesthetic so she'd be ready the instant they showed. Her heart continued to thump a strong, steady rhythm before the woman knocked on her door ten minutes later.

"I always keep a towel and gloves in my car for such a reason, thank goodness," the woman explained. "Thank you so much for taking him in. I'm Katie, by the way."

"Let's see what we have here." Sadie gently took the bundle wrapped in a brown towel from Katie and placed it on the table.

"The truck in front of me swerved—unintentionally, I hope —and clipped the animal's behind," she said.

"We'll see if we can help him."

Concern wrinkled Katie's forehead. "I sure hope you can save him."

"That's always the goal."

The subdued groundhog allowed Sadie to peel away the towel to examine the wound. The groundhog turned out to be female, and she watched Sadie with wary eyes. Sadie kept one hand on her back, stroking the fur while she studied the nasty case of road rash on the animal's hip. Then, she moved the joint slowly to test the pain level, watching for a reaction.

Nothing.

Either she was in shock and the adrenaline had dulled the pain, or the poor thing was paralyzed. She picked up her needle to give it a dose of pain meds. She'd treat the rash with antibiotics and place her in a cage to get her somewhat settled. The pain meds would work their magic, and she'd examine her more thoroughly later.

The woman watched silently, her arms crossed until Sadie transferred the animal to a clean, empty cage.

"I'd like to write you a check if that's okay," Katie offered.

"Donations are always appreciated." Sadie cleaned up the table, throwing the dirty towel in the basket and laying down a new one for the next patient.

"I know rescues live on shoestring budgets. I follow several organizations, including yours, on social media." The woman tore out a check and handed it over to Sadie. "You people do amazing work."

"I appreciate it. This helps quite a bit." She tucked the check into her pocket, making a mental note to add it to the deposit bag for her next trip to the bank.

"I love your photos, by the way," Katie went on. "They're such eye-openers to what you do on a daily basis."

"Thank you. That's the intention."

"It really is a round-the-clock job, isn't it? I had no idea."

Thanks to Cara, Furever Friends Rescue now had a vibrant online presence, something Sadie had always struggled with. Cara, on the other hand, ran with the task. She posted photos of their patients, Sadie treating them, general PSAs about wildlife, and fun trivia. Their followers had grown tenfold during the first month Cara was on board. She'd convinced Sadie to help plan their first outreach event at a local festival right off the bat.

"I noticed that you recently added a wish list on your website. I'll keep that in mind when my birthday rolls around. I like to give to charity to mark the occasion"

"I love that idea. Thank you." As grateful as she felt for the woman's donation and her taking the time to bring the groundhog to her, Sadie struggled with making small talk. She wished to be alone.

The woman finally said goodbye. Across the room, the groundhog rested comfortably on the fleece pad while still keeping one sleepy eye on her.

"You're safe now, buddy," she whispered. "We'll get you fixed up in no time."

\* \* \*

Later that afternoon, Sadie re-examined the groundhog, whom she'd named Katie after her benefactor. She'd administered an anesthetic to examine her more closely. The animal grew groggy enough in no time, allowing Sadie to move the joints to test for mobility. She didn't notice anything off, a good sign, but it was still too early to tell. She peeled back the pad on her wound for a quick peek as Hayes walked into the room with a camera slung around his neck.

"Hey there," he said. "New patient?"

Sadie shot him a quick smile, nodded, then refocused on Katie, though the image of his wind-whipped dark hair left her a little breathless. Sadie thanked the heavens she had something to keep her occupied at the moment.

She replaced the bandage with a clean one then closed the cage door, stepping back so Hayes could get a better view.

"Meet Katie," she said.

He came closer and Sadie caught a hint of woodsmoke and sage.

"What happened?" he asked.

She crumpled up the old dressing and tossed it in the garbage can across the room. "Not sure exactly. Road rash for sure. We think she got bumped by a passing car or maybe took a tumble trying to get out of the way."

"So, internal injuries?"

"It doesn't appear so, but right now I'm giving her pain meds and letting her rest until the morning. Then I'll check her again."

Hayes patted the camera hanging from his neck. "Would you mind? Cara asked me to take some photos for new posts."

She hated when Cara took her photo, or when anyone did

for that matter, but this would be a whole new level of self-consciousness with Hayes behind the lens.

"Not at all. Go for it." Her face had already flushed.

Every second felt forced even though she'd changed bandages a thousand times, administered medications, and replaced containers with fresh water and food. The only sound was the constant clicking of the shutter, though she'd have preferred he talked while he moved around the room. She needed something to calm her nerves.

Besides, Sadie liked listening to him.

The places he'd been while he'd served as an intelligence officer in the Marines boggled her mind. The UK. Germany. Italy. Afghanistan. Turkey. Yemen. There were at least a dozen more he mentioned over dinner in Cara's cabin the other night, but she couldn't think of them now, not with him clicking away, focused on *her*.

"Have you always wanted to work in the rescue business?" he asked finally. He stopped to fiddle with the settings on his camera.

"As long as I've known it was possible."

"Which was when?"

"When I was a kid, there was a woman that lived near my parents' house. My sister Janie actually lives in her house now. Anyway, this woman didn't run a legit rescue. I mean, she didn't advertise it like I do with a sign out front or a page on social media. Who knows, maybe she wasn't even licensed. But one day I found a joey—"

"A joey?"

"A baby opossum."

"Got it. My first thought was a kangaroo." Hayes nodded. "Sorry. Go on."

She smiled at the thought of finding a kangaroo baby in eastern Iowa. "My mom said, 'Let's call Mrs. Vernstotter.' So I wrapped this tiny little thing in a dish towel and my mom walked me over to her house."

"I'm already getting Dr. Doolittle vibes," Hayes said as he lifted the camera to peer through the finder again.

"That's not too far from the truth. She had a giant raccoon curled up on a dog bed in the corner. A raven perched on a rafter above our heads."

"She sounds like a kindred spirit, no?"

She smiled, remembering how transfixed she'd felt the moment she walked into Verna's makeshift animal hospital. It was like she was *home*.

"Definitely. Watching her handle the joey, turning him over to point out his full belly, then nestle him into a fleece pad with a heating lamp pointed at his little body, that's when I knew what I wanted to do." The camera *whirred* and clicked again, so she focused on the two squirrel babies that had come in last month.

For youngsters, they were now pretty calm. Sadie scooped one up from the corner of its cage, careful to shield the open door as best she could to avoid another escape. She offered the already full syringe to it, careful to not release too much fluid into its mouth at once. Once the baby got a taste of the formula, it didn't budge. The look in her eyes had transformed from frantic to resigned, maybe even grateful.

"And you were how old when you brought this woman the opossum?" Hayes asked.

"About ten."

"So that was always the plan, to start your own rescue?"

"Well," she started, giving him a sidelong glance, "eventually

I found out there was no money in it. I interned with a local vet my senior year in high school, you know, one of those job shadow opportunities you can do to earn credit?"

Hayes slipped the camera over his head and set it on the counter behind him. He leaned against the refrigerator, his attention now solely on her. Sadie preferred the camera against his face.

"I shadowed a construction foreman in high school. Learned more there than I did from any books," he said. "Some things you just have to dive into."

"Agreed. What I learned during that semester was that if I wanted to run a rescue, I needed to supplement the expense with a more lucrative job. 'Okay,' I thought, 'I'll study to be a vet.'" She shook her head. "Wrong. The vet I worked under told me the job consumed her. You're on call at all hours, especially in a more populated area. Running a rescue, she'd said, is time-consuming, too. There won't be enough hours in a day to do both *well*."

Hayes crossed his arms, now fully engrossed in their conversation. His laser-focused attention annoyed her, but at the same time, made her chest flutter with nervous energy. She wished he'd pick up his camera again so there was a buffer between them. She liked flying under everyone's radar, always had. She didn't seek attention, and did her best to shy away from it when a spotlight landed on her, in a group conversation outside of her small, intimate circle of family and friends, or when someone from the press wanted more information about the rescue. But here was Hayes, asking questions that didn't feel intrusive or awkward, questions that seemed like he was interested in *her*. It was unnerving, only because she wasn't used to it. With him, she felt *seen*.

This couldn't feel more natural than if she'd known him all her life. Is this what a real relationship should feel like? Like talking to your best friend?

"So, that was when you decided vet school wasn't for you?" Hayes asked.

Sadie feigned a frown. "Not quite. I didn't take the advice at first. I'm a little stubborn."

He chuckled. "I don't believe it."

"I'd made up my mind to be a veterinarian so long ago, that I couldn't let go of that dream."

"Tenacious. I like it," he said with the same earnest smile that made her heart stutter.

Sadie concentrated on feeding the squirrel, watching the end of the syringe wet its lips with formula, while Hayes' words played on repeat in her head.

He liked her tenacity.

But what she really heard was, I like *you*.

*Wait.*

She had no business thinking that. After searching long and hard for a partner to share in the rescue work, the last thing she wanted was to overstep a boundary. Joining forces with Cara had been her mission, a good move for growing the rescue. Getting romantically tangled with Hayes could tip the apple cart.

*Obliterate the cart and make applesauce of its contents was more like it.*

Sadie's eyes pricked with moisture. The longer he stood there watching her, the more her self-consciousness grew. That these thoughts swirled in her mind made it worse.

No, she'd double down on keeping it professional. It wasn't like Hayes had shown signs that he was attracted to her anyway.

Hayes was a good listener, but that came with the job. He was around to help while Cara healed, that was it.

She laughed.

*Look at you. Romantically involved with Hayes? What planet are you living on?*

Hayes was no more interested in her than he was in sticking around Port Chance permanently. He'd look after his sister while she recuperated, then he'd be gone. Blue eyes and charm aside, getting closer to Hayes was just another means to a heartache. She didn't have the grit to go through that again.

*Ever.*

# Chapter Twelve

C ara had recommended the Daily Grind in downtown Port Chance as a place for Hayes to talk with the headhunter who'd reached out the other day. When he pushed open the red Tudor door with the half-moon window and stepped into the quaint but spacious café a few mornings later, he couldn't agree with Cara more. Any of the intimate rooms, repurposed walk-in closets by the looks of them, jutting off from the main seating area were perfect for meeting with Ulla Kraal, the recruiter from Adwell Search Consultants out of Des Moines.

He'd come early to grab a drink, but as he stood at the counter, he felt someone touch his arm. Ulla had arrived even earlier.

"Hayes Kelley, right?" she asked, withdrawing her hand. "I've already found us a table and took the liberty of ordering us a pot of coffee."

They settled into the tiniest of alcoves where she'd tucked them away from the steady stream of customers.

"Port Chance is such a charming town. I had no idea," Ulla

said as she floated a napkin onto her lap. "Have you lived here long?"

"A couple of weeks."

Her eyes popped.

"What made you settle here? Are you a local?" she asked as she poured cream from a diminutive silver pitcher into her mug.

"No, my sister lives here. I'm staying with her temporarily."

"It's a nice area, though I can't say I've ever stopped," she said. "It's one of those places that seem to be too close to my starting or stopping points. I mostly just pass by on the interstate." When she set the pitcher down, a set of silver bangles clattered against the tabletop as she picked up her coffee to sip.

Hayes nodded. "Des Moines is a little like that for me. I always stop before or after I get through town to avoid the congestion." He regretted mentioning that as Ulla's smile faltered.

"Are you open to considering the position in the Des Moines plant, or only the one near Muscatine?" She looked at him over her cup again as she took another sip. Her brown eyes lingered a second too long, waiting for his response. When she set her mug down this time, she toyed with the pendant on her necklace.

"Honestly, I'd prefer Muscatine," he said. "But if Des Moines is interested, I can be flexible."

"Des Moines has a lot to offer. I'd be happy to show you around if it works out," she said, while making figure eights on the corner of the legal pad with her pen.

*Uh oh.* He'd have to tread carefully.

"I might take you up on that," he said in a neutral tone, scanning the café at the same time. There was a line four deep at the counter. The two young ladies behind the counter filled orders as quickly as they could without ricocheting off each other.

Ulla pushed her business card across the table toward him, tapping it with her finger. "Don't be afraid to reach out. *Anytime*."

He shot her a quick smile, keeping their eye contact to a minimum. No need to give her any false hope.

The line grew even longer as the door chimes signaled more customers. He glanced at the small group who'd just walked in, and he almost choked on his drink.

*Sadie*.

Her sister, Kit, the one he'd met at that bakery just down the street, and another woman stood on either side of Sadie.

Kit noticed him before Sadie did, that is until Kit's exuberant wave caught her sister's attention. When Sadie spotted him, her quick smile fell when she noted Ulla's presence, too, in the cozy alcove. Kit, on the other hand, headed over, her gaze bouncing back and forth between him and his companion.

"Hi there, Hayes. You're just enjoying all the special spots in town, aren't you? First the bakery, now this place," Kit chirped.

"My sister recommended the place," he said. "It's nice to have connections, I guess."

Kit bobbed her head in agreement. "We love Cara to pieces. Oh, have you tried the ginger snapless bars?" Kit pressed her palm against her chest. "You'll think you've died and gone to sugar heaven."

"Intriguing name," said Ulla with a tight smile.

Hayes didn't remember Kit being this chatty the first time.

"They're my sister's favorite treat here," she added with a glance at Ulla. Kit waved Sadie over to the table, but Sadie turned her back to them, whispering something to the woman next to her. They stepped toward the front counter to order. The dark mood transforming Sadie's normally neutral expression into one of pure vexation was unmistakable.

"Looks like they're on a mission before they sell out," Ulla stated, picking up her legal pad and giving it a little shake. *A hint.*

Sharp-eyed Kit seemed to get it. "I didn't mean to interrupt. Just wanted to say hi. Now, I'd better go rein Sadie in before she clears the case."

Hayes's attention gravitated toward Sadie as Ulla resumed her questioning. Even facing the baristas, Sadie's stiff posture spoke volumes. Desperate for Ulla to pause and pour herself more coffee or use the restroom, Hayes cleared his throat.

"Do you mind if I grab one of those bars she mentioned? Can I get you one, too?"

Ulla's expression fell before she nodded. "That would be lovely."

Standing shoulder to shoulder with Sadie a second later, Hayes nudged her arm with his elbow.

"Great minds think alike, huh?"

She barely made eye contact. "Yep."

On the opposite side of Sadie, Kit peeked around her sister at him, cocking her brow.

He leaned closer and spoke in an undertone. "I'm trying one of those ginger bars. Kit says they're your favorite?"

Sadie's head shifted toward Kit. He couldn't see the look they exchanged, but judging by Kit's expression, Sadie didn't appreciate the shared knowledge.

"Yes," she said simply.

Clipped tone. Stiff posture. She didn't need to spell it out for him. He could read the signs. Their last encounter was still fresh in his memory. He stood there, recalling snippets of it while he waited his turn. Nothing he remembered could have triggered this frosty response.

When the barista finished serving Sadie and her sister, Kit threw him an apologetic smile on their way past him.

*Okay, it's not just me.* Kit picked up on Sadie's aloof vibe, too.

Maybe it was wishful thinking but he'd hoped their budding friendship would grow into something more. Whatever offense he'd committed in Sadie's mind, Hayes vowed to get to the bottom of it soon.

## Chapter Thirteen

"What's your issue with Hayes?"

Kit's expression looked more comical than cross with pastry crumbs clinging to her bottom lip. Sadie didn't bother pointing this out as they sat in Kit's car with warm air rushing out of the vents. Kit would just accuse her of trying to change the subject. In the backseat, her good friend Rory Hilt alternated between sampling a ginger bar and sipping a white chocolate mocha. Sadie interpreted her grunt to mean she wondered the same thing.

"I don't have any issues with him. I'm in a hurry this morning is all. No time for chitchat."

Kit huffed. "We were literally waiting in line. Chatting or not chatting wasn't going to make the line move any faster."

She stifled a frustrated sigh. "I didn't feel like talking. There's no need to read into it any more than that," she added after a pause. In her peripheral vision, Kit acknowledged that with a nod.

"How's Cara doing?" Rory asked. She leaned forward to direct one of the vents in her direction.

Sadie lifted a shoulder. "Fine, I guess. She's understandably restless."

"And Hayes is staying until when?" Kit brushed her fingers into the pastry bag, then crumbled it.

"At least until she's able to put weight on her foot." She shrugged again. "He's in between jobs now so he's flexible."

Rory settled back against her seat. "That's the bright side of an unfortunate situation. I'm sure this guy will be a big help around the shelter."

"I don't need the help." She'd jumped in with that too quickly. After a moment, she spoke again in a softer tone. "I worked by myself for a long time before Cara came on board."

"You might as well take advantage of him being around," Rory countered. "A big guy like that? I'd let him do all the heavy lifting if I were you."

"I agree," Kit piped in.

She snorted. "Seriously? Kit, that doesn't even sound like you. You've always prided yourself on working harder than anyone you know. Invincible Kit can do anything and everything, and I'm the same way."

Kit shot her a sympathetic look. "That was my problem. Pride."

"I don't see it as a problem, wanting to be independent." She relaxed her shoulders when a tightness crept into her neck muscles.

"Being independent isn't what this is about," Kit said.

She let her head fall back against the seat. "Sorry, not following."

Silence filled the car. *Good. Didn't like where it was heading anyway.*

"Not every man is like Evan," Kit said finally.

That familiar grip closed around her heart, more faintly than it used to, but it still made its presence known. Her ex-husband had woven his way into the fabric of her life, and she hated that those poison-laced threads still affected her well-being.

"I know that."

Her fingers dug into the edge of her seat. Rory shifted behind her but stayed silent. Rory had endured many days listening to Sadie decompress during the downfall of her marriage to Evan. Kit hadn't been around for it, traveling the country, taking odd jobs just to get by. Having the time of her life, no doubt.

*Me? Not so much.*

"Do you?" Kit asked, wide-eyed.

"Sure, I do. But I don't need to prove it by letting some strange guy carry feed bags for me. I'm sure he's a peach, but I'll get along just fine until Cara's well."

Kit put the car in reverse with an exaggerated frown. "All I'm saying is don't be so quick to turn him down."

*Turn him down.*

Maybe Kit meant his offers to help, but all Sadie heard were the echoing refrains from her mother and sisters: *it's time to get back out there.*

They drove in silence through Port Chance, dropping Rory off at home, and continued on to their parents' neighborhood on the east side of town. Their childhood home, a quaint Victorian with lush, expansive gardens thanks to Sonia Wendell's green thumb, welcomed them as they turned into the winding, pea gravel driveway. This time of year the gardens slept under a blanket of decaying leaves and newly fallen snow. Aaron Wendell's cutout reindeer stood in all their plywood glory around the lawn, draped with string lights that would light up the yard at dusk. She and Kit had come to pick up Dad's latest contribution to the rescue: a plywood fox pair Sadie would place in front of the intake building year round.

Kit stopped the car in front of their father's workshop, the old garage he now used for his woodworking hobby. Its little chimney emitted a thin trail of white smoke into the overcast sky, a sign Dad had lit the cast-iron stove inside.

"I'm sorry for upsetting you," Kit said.

Sadie stared straight ahead. Her father's figure moved around inside the workshop. He came to the window, gave a tentative wave, then disappeared again.

"You didn't. It's been a tough few days at the rescue is all. I lost a couple animals that I hadn't expected to."

"I'm sorry," Kit said, then took Sadie's hand for a quick squeeze.

"Comes with the job, I guess." A tightness took hold of her throat, but she swallowed it down. "I'm just out of sorts."

Kit took a deep breath and exhaled through her nose.

"We're more alike than you realize." Kit put her hand up when Sadie chuckled deep in her throat. "I know, I know. That might be a stretch."

"I know what you mean. Stoic. Resilient." She smiled at Kit, appreciating the effort Kit made to empathize. Heart-to-heart talks didn't come naturally to her younger sister. "At least by all outward appearances, right?"

"Mom and Dad had their work cut out for them when we were growing up, didn't they?" Kit chuckled, unbuckling her seatbelt.

"Having Nana and Pops around probably kept them sane."

Sadie turned up her collar at the same time their father appeared in the workshop's doorway. He gave them a hearty wave.

What her sister didn't realize was that Kit's independent nature had been baked into her DNA since birth, but that wasn't so with Sadie.

She'd been a timid, clingy child until high school when, by some cruel twist of fate, her future husband noticed her. Evan Grassey had transformed from a gangly class clown into a cocky and boisterous dreamboat overnight. In him, she saw some of the qualities she wished for herself. He was confident and well-liked, not anything like the average, socially awkward girl she saw in the mirror. But their relationship changed her.

When the most popular guy in school attached himself to her and her fragile teenaged psyche, they were too naïve to know their relationship was built on false assumptions. She was too lovesick to know he wasn't worthy of all the admiration heaped on him by his peers. He, in turn, was too busy basking in his fandom to realize she was one of the last people who belonged in his orbit.

No, her independence had been built on tears and empty promises. Thanks to Evan, Sadie promised herself to never make the same mistake twice—handing her heart to someone who didn't deserve it.

Over time, she'd also started to believe maybe no one did.

*Chapter Fourteen*

H ayes turned off the highway and into the driveway of Furever Friends later that afternoon. The sun had finally broken through the downy gray clouds overhead. A spot of blue hovered on the horizon to the west, a hopeful promise of brighter days ahead.

Two life-sized cutouts of a fox pair stood near the front door of the intake building. Wrapped in Christmas lights, they were a cheery addition to the otherwise stark white surroundings. He smiled.

As he parked the truck in front of the cabin, Sadie appeared in the doorway of the carriage house toward the back of the property, oblivious of his arrival. Her long down coat concealed the trim figure that had fooled him into thinking she wasn't as hardy as she appeared when they first met. Now, wearing a woven Nordic cap with colorful twin braids dangling near her ears, Sadie looked like some of his Scandinavian cousins pictured in the photo albums his mother had painstakingly gathered from their European connections over the years.

Sadie hoisted a long, narrow box over one shoulder and

trudged down the driveway toward her house. She stopped and shifted the load before continuing on her way until she pushed the awkward container too far back. It teetered while she struggled to right it, but then it fell from her shoulder and onto the ground. Her muffled exclamation carried across the way and into the confines of his truck.

"Need a hand?" he called as he opened the truck door.

She startled and looked up.

"No?" Sadie answered quickly, sounding a little annoyed.

Hayes continued up the sloping drive. "You don't sound very convincing," he called.

The scowl she'd worn at the Daily Grind was back, growing deeper with each step he took toward her.

"I've got it," she insisted. "It's not heavy, only awkward."

He stooped to lift it. She was right. It wasn't heavy, but the box's size made it cumbersome to carry. The thing rested squarely on his shoulder as he secured it with one arm.

"Where do you want it?"

"Hayes, I said—"

He swiveled to see her rooted to the spot, hands on her hips.

"I know what you said. Is it that hard for you to accept a hand?" His tone was light, but it stung a little to be rejected for every offer to help lately.

Her lips clamped together, turning pale, but she didn't move.

He let the box slide back to the ground before he put his hands up to surrender.

"Fine," he said. "There you go. Have a good rest of your day."

Hayes started his walk back to the cabin. The detour to help her wasn't the best idea in hindsight. He'd already resigned himself to not earning a spot in her inner circle, but sometimes it took more than one rejection to get through his thick-skulled ideals.

"Hayes."

He stopped. Behind him, Sadie's boots crunched on the snow as she drew closer.

"I'm sorry. I'm out of practice," she said.

When he turned, Sadie's expression was one part apologetic and one part sorrowful. The stark landscape made her eyes look more green than hazel. He drew in a sharp breath.

"The box belongs in my cabin. I'd appreciate it if you brought it there," she added with a halfhearted grin.

He retraced his steps, threw the box over his shoulder, and nodded. "I'd be happy to."

She led the way down the driveway and across a trail paved with stone slabs to the wide front porch of her cabin. Her home was three times the size of Cara's place, and looked newer, too. Sadie held the door open, then directed him to set the box near the immense, two-story flagstone fireplace on the other side of the room. Soaring ceilings and a loft gave it an airy feel, but the richly polished pine logs created a warm, welcoming atmosphere.

"It's much bigger than I need," she said when she noticed him gaping. "When I bought it, I thought...well, maybe someday I'll sell and move to something smaller."

"It's beautiful. I'd have a hard time parting with it." He looked around. "Is right here okay?"

She pushed an overstuffed crimson armchair a few feet to make room before pointing to the empty spot near the fireplace.

"Would you like help setting this up? I'm somewhat of a pro."

Sadie shook her head before he finished speaking, then caught herself in the act. Her shoulders slumped as she caught his eye.

"No, thanks. You've done enough." She tugged off her hat to toss it onto the couch. "It's...it's not you. I'm just beat, so I'll save it for another day."

He stuffed his hands in his pockets and let out a deep sigh. "Well, you know where I am, so give me a shout."

Sadie walked him to the door and placed her hand on the knob but didn't open it for him. Their eyes met for a split second, but it was enough to set his skin simmering.

"Did you order the ginger bar today?" she asked in a soft voice. Her gaze flitted away then locked on him again.

"I did. It was as good as Kit claimed it to be." Her demeanor had changed. She seemed more skittish, unsure of herself.

She tucked a strand of hair behind her ear that had fallen forward, wrapping itself underneath her chin.

"Was I...I mean, if I was rude..."

"You weren't." That wasn't the whole truth, but now wasn't the time to debate it. "Sometimes I forget to gate check my obnoxiousness in public."

Sadie shot him a skeptical look. "You're hardly obnoxious. The second child usually wins in that department. Take Kit and Cara, for example."

"I'd rather not." He gritted his teeth then chuckled under his breath.

"Anyway, it's been a tough few days, and I took my mood out on you."

"I get it. I've seen how rehab work sometimes affects Cara, too."

"That doesn't make it right," she said as her forehead creased.

He nodded. Sadie's earnest expression looked like she had more to say.

"Sometimes I wonder if this is the right path for me. I mean, deep down, I know it is," she mused. "But some days are more uncertain than others." Sadie clamped her lips together like she hadn't meant to share so much.

"If it makes you feel better, my sister is happy here. She says you're one of the more passionate and professional rehabbers she's worked with."

Sadie smiled and looked down at her feet. "That's good to hear."

"So, what changes day to day?" he asked softly.

"When I first started rehabbing, it was like the North Star guided me. Everything felt *right.*"

"Then what happened?"

She chuckled humorlessly. "The rose-colored glasses came off. I mean, I knew it'd be tough, that I'd see things that would break my heart."

"And you've had a few of those days recently."

She nodded and looked down at her shoes again. Her lip quivered until she stopped it by biting down.

Instinctively, he stepped forward, closing the space between them with a long stride. Without thinking, his arms were around her—one against her shoulder blades, the other around her waist. Sadie stiffened, but she didn't pull away. For a split second, the length of their bodies pressed together, squeezing the breath from his lungs. It stole his voice, too, when he tried to speak.

An apology was on his lips even before he stepped back again. "I'm sorry—"

"It's all right. You don't have to—" Confusion clouded her flushed face.

Hayes's nerves hummed at his impulsiveness, yet he wished he hadn't pulled away so quickly. Prolonging the hug would've been a jerk move for taking advantage of her misery, though.

"What I mean is, I'm sorry you're feeling this way," he said in a rush. *I'm not sorry for hugging you.*

"Oh..."

He inhaled deeply. "Putting your soul into this only to see what cruelty people are capable of. That's hard." He'd better stop talking lest he make a bigger fool of himself.

"Yes."

"But your work matters," he went on. Flustered, he couldn't stop the flow of nonsense coming out of his mouth. "Most people know that."

*I have no idea what I'm talking about.* At least Sadie was gracious enough to not call him out on it.

She nodded again, flicking the corner of her eye. "I'm sorry."

"Sadie?"

Her hand dropped to her side and she looked at him expectantly, blinking.

"That's two apologies today. There's no reason for it."

He reached for the doorknob, but when his hand closed over the top of hers, they both jumped like they'd been scalded.

"Sorry," he said while the sensation of her finely boned hand underneath his palm caused another shiver to skitter across the back of his neck.

Nervousness tinged Sadie's laughter. "Look who's apologizing now."

"I'd better leave before we meet our quota for the week," he said after he'd gathered his breath.

"That's probably a good idea."

Outside, the waning light cast long shadows underneath his feet. Despite the cold and the days growing steadily darker, there was a lightness in his step he hadn't noticed in a long time.

## Chapter Fifteen

Sadie waited until Hayes's truck disappeared down the driveway the next morning before she carried the foil-wrapped plate of cinnamon coffee cake to Cara's cabin. It'd been ages since she'd baked anything, but the urge had come over her last night, and miraculously she'd found every ingredient in her pantry.

She wished he hadn't apologized for hugging her. That meant he thought it was a mistake. On the contrary, his gesture meant the world to her, a soothing elixir. It made her feel comfortable and *safe*. But of course she'd spent the whole night overthinking it and was now convinced Hayes only felt sorry for her. Now, the hug felt wrong, given to her out of pity.

Sadie didn't need anyone pitying her.

*But oh, how his arms felt around me, even for the tiniest moment.*

Sadie closed her eyes as she paused on the porch before knocking. Was it her imagination or did his cologne still linger here outside the door?

*Stop before you do something stupid like start dreaming about the guy.*

Wasn't it already too late?

Sadie knocked in a hurry before she could answer that.

Cara called, "Come in!" on the other side of the door.

Inside, Cara sat in her usual spot on the couch, her laptop resting on her legs.

"What did I do to earn this?" Cara asked when Sadie presented her the plate. She peeled back the foil. Her brows rose in a slow arch as she plucked a bite-sized square from the plate to sample.

Sadie plunked down in a winged chair across from her. "Thought you could use a pick-me-up."

Cara closed her eyes as she savored the taste. "This is heaven, Sadie. Hayes will be sorry he missed you. I should save him some. He has the biggest sweet tooth."

Sadie remembered this from the other day, standing in line at Daily Grind. She swallowed hard at the mention of Hayes's name. For most of the night she'd dwelled on their time together yesterday. How he'd carried her Christmas tree into the house, offering to help her decorate. How patient he'd been even when she'd been nothing but rude. And then he'd actually *listened* while she spilled her guts. She almost clapped a hand against her forehead in embarrassment, recalling the memory. He'd popped into her thoughts more often lately, and it threw her off-kilter.

"There's plenty there for both of you." Sadie nodded to Cara's foot, which she'd propped up on a tasseled pillow at the end of the futon. "How are you feeling?"

"I can't wait to ditch the crutches. I'm praying the doctor says I'm ready for a walking cast at my next appointment," Cara said. "Hayes is probably praying for that more than I am, though. He's been an angel, but he's getting restless waiting on me."

She pictured Hayes doting on his sister, and warmth spread upward from her neck. Compassion ran in their family. He'd come to Sadie's rescue more than once, even after she'd turned him away. She'd try harder to appreciate that part of him. Letting him help around here didn't mean she owed him anything other than her gratitude, right?

She leaned forward. "You'll be ready for the school program at the beginning of December, then?"

Cara nodded. "That's the plan. From what I hear, it'll be cake to get back on my feet wearing the boot once I get used to it. I'll still need the crutches for a week while I acclimate myself." Cara let her head fall against the pillow as she looked at the ceiling. "I'm just so tired of lying around."

Sadie took Cara's water glass to the kitchen to refill it at the refrigerator dispenser. Thank goodness the school program was a go. She'd hate to lose the opportunity, but she'd feared it was in jeopardy when Cara broke her ankle.

While filling the glass, the photos on the refrigerator door drew her attention.

*Hayes and Cara, tanned and sipping drinks with palm trees standing tall in the background.*

*Hayes carrying Cara on his back at some sporting event.*

They didn't look much younger in the photos than they did now. For some reason, their closeness warmed her heart. Probably because she shared the same close relationship with her own sisters.

She scanned the photos, stopping to study a photo of who she guessed were their parents. Hayes shared his father's eyes and his mother's smile. Another photo of Hayes as a teenager posing to pitch a baseball made her smile.

The next photo stopped her breath.

Hayes's casual stance was unpretentious, but that's what made it so captivating. His hands rested on his hips, while the shirt he wore was halfway unbuttoned, stretching across his broad shoulders. His smile was so bright she almost needed sunglasses.

Sadie gulped.

The sun glinted off the top of his dark hair, giving it a halo effect. He appeared to be hamming it up for whomever was behind the camera. She couldn't take her eyes off the photo.

Hayes's movie-star looks hadn't gone to his head, that's for sure. He seemed as down to earth as one could get, given he was easy to look at and brilliant and...

The sound of water leaking from somewhere startled her back to reality. She scanned the room for the source.

*What on earth*...

"Sadie, what's dripping?"

"I have no idea—"

She took a step back from the refrigerator, the glass in her hand, and...*oh*.

A puddle gathered around her feet, fed by the steady stream of water trickling down the front of the appliance. She'd absent-mindedly kept Cara's glass pressed against the dispenser even as it overflowed.

"Look around. It has to be coming from somewhere." Cara sounded a little more frantic.

"Found it. The dispenser was stuck," she lied as she looked around for a towel to sop up the water seeping underneath the refrigerator. She grabbed one hanging from the dishwasher handle, tossing it to the floor. *Geesh. All this because of one little photo? What's my problem?*

"Thank you," Cara said, taking the water glass when Sadie brought it back a moment later. "There are towels in the drawer next to the sink."

She'd need more than one towel.

"What does your family do for Thanksgiving?" Cara asked from the other room as Sadie finished cleaning up the puddle.

She used the last of four towels to dry the floor before joining Cara in the living room, sinking into the chair again. "Everyone brings something. It's usually just our mom and dad and us sisters. Rose's family too, of course. Extended family comes for Christmas, which is a huge deal. What about you?"

"Hayes and I will head home. It's our parents' turn to host this year. Thanksgiving usually rotates amongst our aunts and uncles. Luckily, they're all relatively close by so we don't have to travel very far."

"And how about Christmas?"

"It's more low-key. We'll probably stick around here. Our parents are traveling down to Florida to celebrate with my dad's sister. That is, if Hayes doesn't take a job elsewhere."

A flush rose up her neck. "Do you think there's a chance of that? That he'll be somewhere else by then?"

"I do." Cara made a face.

"No one hires so close to Christmas. I'm betting he'll still be around here in a month."

Cara winced as she repositioned her leg on the pillow.

"That would be ideal, if for no reason other than to help my sorry self get around."

For the first time since Hayes showed his face at Furever Friends, Sadie hoped she was right.

*Chapter Sixteen*

Hayes intentionally parked his truck up the hill from Mowdry's Market to enjoy the first bright day in a week. His boots scuffed along the sidewalk as melting snow dribbled from the eaves above, creating rivulets along the pavement. Across the street, the fogged windows of Daisy Gap Café and a few doors down, Dough Baby Bakery, tempted him with a warm oasis and something to take the edge off his appetite.

What would it hurt to stop in at the bakery to say hi to Sadie's sister, Rose?

*Not a thing.*

If one of Sadie's other sisters happened to be there too, well, what a coincidence. He'd visit while he grabbed a bag of pastries. With luck, maybe someone would mention Sadie, how she told them what a generous guy he was for helping her move Christmas decor the other day. Or that she's so thankful to have an extra hand around the shelter since Cara is laid up.

*At least your sense of humor is intact.*

Sadie giving him a second thought, let alone mentioning

him to her sisters, was a delusion. The sooner he accepted that fact the better off he'd be. His impulse to hug her yesterday seemed like the right move at the time, but the more he dwelled on it, the more wrong it felt. Had he comforted her for her own good or his? He'd been second-guessing himself all morning long.

And what had she said without hesitation when he mentioned leaving? *It's probably a good idea,* she'd said.

If she didn't have a good reason to avoid him before, she did now.

So he'd stay on this side of the street without a second glance toward the bakery window painted with a wintry theme of snowflakes and holly. Cara had sent him on a mission to buy ingredients at the market for the apple-cranberry pie she planned to make for Thanksgiving anyway.

*Strike that.* The pie she'd *coach* him on making from the comfort of a kitchen chair.

"You're a shiny new face in an otherwise ordinary day."

Hayes slowed his steps, looking around for the source of the ragged voice.

"Don't tell me that side of the street is more interesting than this one."

He'd narrowed the direction down to somewhere underneath the low porch roof of the antique store he now stood in front of. Hayes peered upward for the shop name. The sun glinted off the etched metal signage: The Shoppe of Curious Goods.

"I wouldn't dare," Hayes said, matching the note of humor in the man's voice. "Just wondering how they manage to stay open with you stealing all their business."

The man's throaty laugh seemed to surround Hayes. But

then a crooked figure emerged from behind a life-sized vintage plastic Santa standing next to the sidewalk. His sunny smile matched St. Nick's.

"I won't be getting any business if I can't get Chubby here to light up again," the man said, flicking Santa's nose with his finger.

"Let me take a look."

Hayes knelt next to the plastic figure, checking the connection near one of its boots. The man stood over him, hands planted on both knees. His noisy breath was a steady rhythm in Hayes's ear.

"This is an easy fix. The neutral wire is worn out." Hayes stood. "I can swap it out in about five minutes."

"How much?" The man squinted through one rheumy gray eye.

"A new circuit will cost no more than a few bucks."

"You can do it?"

"Yessir."

The man swept his cap off his head to give it a good rubbing. "John Goodwin. Friends call me Jumpin'."

"Hayes Kelley. Good to meet you. I have to ask, though. Jumpin'?"

"Long jump state champ. Class of '72. My friends could have come up with a worse nickname."

"True. That's quite the accomplishment."

The man chuckled. "I peaked early in life. Haven't done a lick since. Are you new to town?" Jumpin' asked.

"Sort of." He laughed when the guy shot him a quizzical look. "It's temporary. I'm between jobs and staying at my sister's place out at the wildlife rescue."

Jumpin' squinted again, suspicious. "Sadie Wendell? There

are only girls in the Wendell family. No brothers that I'm aware of."

"Sorry. Her partner, Cara Ortega. Cara's my sister."

A light when on. "Got it. Sometimes I'm a little thick." He gave his own head a little finger flick. "Why don't you come inside? I'll give you my card. Give me a shout when you'll be back to fix Mr. Claus."

Hayes followed him inside the shop. The lighting wasn't the best, but this guy sure had a variety of old stuff. Furniture and display cases lined the narrow aisles like silent sentries, and knickknacks littered every available surface. Old metal signs decorated the walls, and in the spirit of the season, there was a good deal of Christmas decor, too.

"Have a look around if you'd like," Jumpin' urged.

Hayes nodded, tucked his hands in his coat pocket, and set off down the first aisle. Cara didn't expect him back any time soon, so he could spare a few minutes to walk through this guy's shop. Hayes might very well be his first customer of the day. He was probably lonely.

Jumpin' followed him at first, commenting on random pieces like a museum docent. He stopped in front of a faceless mannequin dressed in an early-twentieth-century lounge jacket and trousers. A crimson vest and paisley tie finished the outfit, but everything looked stiff and uncomfortable.

"Found this at an estate sale in West Liberty. It'd been stuffed in a trunk in a farmhouse attic for a century. Pristine condition. " He took the bowler hat off the mannequin's head to plop on his own. "Too *frou frou* for my tastes, but I like hats."

Jumpin' also pointed out a lidded red cloisonné vase. "Dellie's gonna see this and take it the first chance she gets. The hummingbirds are pretty, no?"

"Very nice. Dellie?"

"My daughter," Jumpin' said. He replaced the hat on top of the mannequin's head. "She has her own shop in Rock Island."

The old man eventually wandered back to the front of the shop when the door bells jingled a greeting to a new customer.

Halfway down the second aisle Hayes stopped in front of an artificial Christmas tree. An assortment of ornaments hung from the branches—bottlebrush animals, yarn-wrapped God's eye crosses, a random selection of Peanuts-themed figurines. The non-theme oddly worked. Hayes unhooked a raccoon from a branch. He'd buy it for Cara.

He wound through the remaining aisles so he could say he'd seen it all if Jumpin' put him on the spot, but paused again in front of a rattan chair. A rustic metal star was propped against the chair back. Even with rust spots speckling two of its points, it was in good shape.

*When I first started rehabbing, it was like the North Star guided me.*

The wistful look Sadie wore when she said that had mesmerized him.

That star was going home with him.

"Find something?" Jumpin' asked when Hayes set it down on the counter a few minutes later. The old man held it up like it was a priceless piece of art. "Is it for you?"

Hayes shook his head as he slipped out his wallet.

Jumpin' held up his hand. "How about a swap instead? The star in exchange for you fixing Chubby outside for me."

"I think I'm getting the better part of the deal," he said as he remembered the raccoon ornament in his hand that he'd picked out for Cara. He set it on the counter, too, but Jumpin' waved away his second attempt to pay.

"Maybe that's the point," Jumpin' said with a merry grin.

"Sorry, I don't follow."

"Guilt will get you back here sooner rather than later."

The man was a wily one. Hayes liked him.

Jumpin' handed the star back to him. "If my addled brain is remembering right, this came from the estate of a woman who owned a Christmas tree farm. She had this hanging above the barn door."

"Whereabouts was the farm?"

Jumpin' gave him a one-sided smile. "Up north somewhere."

A tingle raced up Hayes's spine.

Sadie's North Star. This was the definition of serendipity right here, a revelation so clear he wished he could share it without sounding like he'd lost it.

"Do you have a place for it?" Jumpin' asked.

Hayes ran his hand over the rough surface. He could spruce it up with a fresh coat of silver enamel paint, but he kind of liked its imperfections.

"I know the perfect spot," Hayes said with a decisive nod.

*Chapter Seventeen*

A few days later, Sadie spent the better part of the morning updating the shelter's wish list at the request of Jed Killeen for his daughter's school fundraiser. The process felt awkward. Engaging with the public was a big reason she'd hired Cara. Asking strangers to donate felt close to begging, which is why she struggled to add supplies to this online list.

She perched on a stool at her kitchen counter, searching for milk replacer powders, feeding dishes, heating pads, and adhesive bandages. Adding supplies like paper towels and disinfectant felt especially wrong, like she was taking advantage of Jed's generosity. But Cara had scolded her the day before when Sadie reluctantly shared the list with her.

"Those are the supplies you run out of all the time. If someone is willing to donate these things, let them!" Cara had laughed when Sadie helplessly slumped in her chair. "The days of you paying for everything out of your own pocket are over, my dear," Cara said.

So she'd added more items to the wish list at Cara's insistence, but when she forwarded the link to Jed, he'd called her almost immediately.

"There needs to be more added to this list," he'd said. "Over one hundred fifty families attend Sycamore Elementary. We'll go through this in no time. Think bigger!"

That's what she'd done for the last hour, and now it was time for a break. Surely a list of more than two hundred items was enough. She couldn't imagine that many donations, or the storage space she'd need to accommodate even half of it. If that came to pass, she could think of worse problems to overcome.

Sadie closed her laptop, feeling the effects of staring at a screen too long. A little fresh air would do her good. She grabbed her coat from the hook by the door, shrugged it on, and stepped outside.

It was another beautiful morning. Spots of snow from the last storm still clung to the shaded areas of the property. Fallen acorns and black walnuts, once again exposed, had the squirrels busy as they resumed stocking up for the cold months ahead. Todd the fox paced in his outdoor enclosure, a sign that Cara and Hayes had already finished the morning chores.

As she came around the corner of the intake building, an unfamiliar sound slowed her pace. Sadie stopped to look around.

The metallic pinging grew more frequent as the breeze kicked up a notch. It came from somewhere above her head.

*What on earth?*

Sadie looked up, shielding her eyes from the painfully bright sky. A flash on the wall above the door caught her attention then, and Sadie stepped back to get a better look, puzzled.

A metal star swung gently against the siding.

*Well, hello there.*

Sadie grinned to herself as she studied it.

How it might have ended up there infused her with gratefulness. It unlocked something inside her, almost as if a part of her heart she'd previously closed off had nudged open again.

"What are you smiling about?" Cara asked when Sadie entered the building a few seconds later. Cara was seated at the old oak desk that often served as a makeshift exam table when Sadie worked on some of their smaller patients. Her laptop was open. She'd been scrolling through a gallery of photos.

"Nothing." Sadie took out her water bottle then set her bag on top of the refrigerator. She took a long drink, realizing she hadn't had anything except her morning coffee. No wonder she was parched. A little headache poked at a spot between her eyes, too.

Cara spun around in the rolling chair and eyed her fully.

"No one smiles like that unless she's keeping a juicy secret. Spill it," she pressed.

"There's nothing to tell. Can't I come in here in a good mood?"

Cara snorted. "Of course you can. It's just...unusual."

She shot Cara a sidelong glance and thrust out her bottom lip. "Am I that big of a grump?"

Her partner pulled a sympathetic grin. "I hate to break it to you," she said before mimicking an exaggerated frown.

Across the room, the silver fox named Pepper darted back and forth inside her cage. She stopped to snuffle around the metal bowl for the remnants of her last meal, then resumed her pacing. She wasn't favoring her foreleg as much as she had the other day. Maybe the transition to an outdoor pen would come sooner rather than later. She and Todd might be cage mates if their meet-and-greet went the way Sadie hoped.

Cara stared at her with a half-grin.

"What?" Sadie squirmed under her partner's scrutiny. Were her thoughts swirling around her like an aura, and Cara was in range to read them? Gosh, she hoped not. Her growing feelings for Hayes would create a conflict no one needed.

"I uploaded the photos Hayes took of you last week," Cara finally said in a chipper voice. "Wanna see?"

"Sure." Sadie set down her bottle, then peered over Cara's shoulder, thankful to be away from Cara's prying eyes.

The first photo that popped up was one of Sadie bent over Katie the groundhog. Her hand rested on the animal's side as Sadie gazed at her face. The shot was a portrait of compassion with Hayes's focus on Sadie's soft expression. If he'd shot the photo from another angle, he might have caught the fear in Katie's eyes. Instead, this photo told a different story, one from Sadie's point of view.

There was a close up of Sadie's fingers holding the animal's tiny paw.

Another showed the collection of bottles, syringes, and bandages on the exam table.

A photo of Charles Darwin's framed quote on the wall. *The love for all living creatures is the most noble attribute of man.*

It was the next one that stopped Sadie's breath.

The photo was of her. She was smiling wide, almost laughing. She knew at what point he'd taken the photo. It was during the story she shared about the turkey hen which Sadie cared for years ago after someone found it caught in a barbed wire fence. She'd treated the lacerations on her foot and released her weeks later. But the turkey continued to show up at her front door weekly, and eventually she arrived with the brood of poults she'd hatched during the years. Sadie tried her best not to become attached to these animals. They weren't hers. They belonged in the wild. But she'd loved that turkey.

Hayes had captured her in a way that Sadie didn't recognize herself. She saw joy, hope, and passion in her face. The person in the photo was in love with life.

Was this what Hayes saw in her, too?

"What a great photo," Cara said, bringing Sadie out of her reverie. "I'm using this one on the brochure I'm putting together."

"Yeah?" Sadie answered, still staring at the photo.

"I hate to admit it, but my brother is a better photographer than I am. But don't tell him that. His head is already big enough."

Distracted, Sadie made a small sound in agreement.

Cara pushed away from the desk to stand, reaching for her crutches. "I'll let you finish looking through these. Hayes is taking me to Iowa City to see the orthopedic doctor again. The sooner I can get back to being useful, the better. I'm hoping I don't need surgery.

"You're plenty useful. If you only stayed on to take care of all the outreach stuff, I'd owe you my life."

"I know. I'm just teasing."

Sadie looked down at her cast. "I thought surgery was off the table?"

Cara grimaced. "The X-rays at the two-week follow-up looked like it wasn't healing as quickly as expected. I'm meeting with the doctor today to talk about transitioning from this cast to a brace."

"Good luck." Sadie crossed both sets of fingers. "Oh, by the way, that star outside above the doorway? What's the deal? I know *you* didn't put it up there."

"It was Hayes," Cara said, a ripple of confusion crossing her face. "Didn't you ask him to hang it?"

"Me? No."

"That's funny. When I asked him about it, he said it was yours. Something about your North Star."

She turned away so Cara wouldn't see how a sudden flash of heat reddened her face.

"I might have said something about decorating for the holidays," she said quickly. It was a little fib, but her guilt was offset by the sweetness of Hayes's gesture.

*Her North Star.*

Not only had he listened to her silly ramblings, he'd actually gone out of his way to find a meaningful gift. She swallowed to clear the lump in her throat.

After Cara left, the car's rumble from its ailing muffler growing more faint as it pulled onto the highway, Sadie took her time going through the rest of Hayes's photos. It felt intimate, studying Hayes's work. Seeing herself through his eyes sparked a feeling of connectedness she'd never felt with another person. What did it mean? Had he felt something similar when he'd seen these photos, too?

As soon as Cara's ankle healed, Hayes would be gone. That put it right around New Year's at the latest.

Was it strange that she wanted Hayes to leave and dreaded his inevitable absence at the same time?

*Chapter Eighteen*

One more trip from the cabin to his truck was in order as Hayes carried a steaming casserole dish on Thanksgiving day later that week. The heat penetrated his two oven mitts as he set it gently on the floor of the backseat. In all, two hot dishes, a veggie tray, and a pie crowded the backseat. Cara had volunteered to make the cranberry-apple pie, which had translated to "you bake, and I'll coach you." Two casseroles and the vegetable platter had somehow found their way onto the to-do list since then. They should have left for dinner at their parents' place across the river an hour ago. They'd most likely miss his aunts' rousing game of Scattergories now.

"You're quiet today," Cara said as they waited at the end of the drive to turn onto the highway. "I don't think you've said two words."

He cast one last glance toward Sadie's cabin before it disappeared from view in his rearview mirror.

"There's a lot on my mind right now."

Cara glanced at him. "It's not the news that I need surgery, is it? I'll be fine. The healing journey has been extended a bit, that's all."

"I mean, that's not good news, but I know you'll get there eventually." He draped one wrist over the steering wheel as they came down the hill from the rescue. Ahead, the river appeared above the tree tops. "No, it's work-related."

"Details?"

"I was going to wait until it's finalized, but I got a job offer."

"Hayes, that's great! I can't believe you're holding back." She punched him affectionately on the arm. "Wait, why don't you seem excited?"

"The job will be in Des Moines." He chanced a look. Sure enough, her brows slanted with a frown.

"Des Moines? That's even farther than your last job."

"I'm aware. But it'd be a higher salary and two weeks more of vacation."

Cara chewed her lip, looking straight ahead. "That's great for you, I suppose," she said in a small voice.

"I got two offers actually, but the second one doesn't pay as much."

"Then it sounds like you've already made up your mind." She smiled at him, but it wasn't exactly a heartfelt one. "I'm being selfish. Sorry. I'm happy for you, Hayes. Really."

"Thanks." He reached for her hand and gave it a quick squeeze. She'd made it clear that she hoped he'd end up closer to her and their parents.

"When do you start?"

"First of the year. I told them it'd be a non-starter if they wanted me before then. That way I can stick around for the surgery and part of your recovery."

They inched over the Interstate 80 bridge as holiday traffic and a light snow slowed their progress. His foot hovered over the brake, but the congestion cleared as they neared the Illinois side.

"Did you mention this...to anyone else?" Cara asked.

"I only found out today. I'll tell Mom and Dad sometime in the next week. I don't want the focus on me today."

"And Sadie? Will you tell her?"

Her question caught him off guard.

"I-I guess so?"

In his peripheral vision, Cara nodded.

Why did she think Sadie should know?

In his mind, he'd planned to tell her anyway. But Cara's concern that he share the news with Sadie was odd.

They drove in silence for the next ten minutes until they pulled into Ron and Tammy Kelley's driveway in a tree-lined subdivision. The garage door of their sage-green Cape Cod at the end of the cul-de-sac was open. Smoke emitted from the grill manned by their father. Even at a distance, Dad's traditional buffalo check apron stood out like a fly in the cream. The Grillin' and Chillin' motto on its front wasn't a stretch either. Beer in hand, he embraced the task.

"You look like you're getting around better than the last time we saw you," Dad said to Cara, eyeing her cast while he poked the turkey roasting in a pan on the grill with a meat fork.

Cara laughed as she looped her arms around his neck for a hug. "That was three days ago. Not much happened in between."

"I hear you've got a live-in nurse already lined up." He winked at Hayes. "Did you schedule the surgery yet?"

Cara nodded. "The week before Christmas. Perfect timing," she said sarcastically.

At that moment, Aunt Blythe, looking spry in a wool plaid skirt and crisp blouse, bounded down the short set of steps into the garage, sweeping Cara into a perfume-infused hug. Hayes handed over the pie and one of the casseroles to her outstretched hands.

"Time for visiting later?" She pressed her cheek against his since her arms were now too full for a hug. "We're behind in the kitchen. With luck, dinner will be ready by five. Don't dry that turkey out, you hear, Ronnie?" Aunt Blythe shooed Cara away from them before he had time to answer.

It grew quiet again once Aunt Blythe closed the door.

"Guess who stopped by earlier?" Dad said. He bent over a cooler to retrieve a drink for Hayes, tossing him a can. "Your old buddy, Randy."

"Giving him a call was at the top of my list. Is he back in town for the whole weekend?" He and Randy Meers had been tight in high school. They'd stayed in touch over the years when Randy moved to the East Coast for work, and made a point to get together during the holidays when he visited family.

"He's staying the full week from what he told me." Dad hooked the meat fork on the grill's handle and set the lid back on the roaster. "Man, I miss those days sitting on the bleachers watching you two play ball."

"Me too. Life was certainly simpler then."

"That reminds me. He wondered where you were staying, so I told him about the rehab center. Apparently, he knows Sadie Wendell from years ago."

"Really? Small world."

"Randy said you'd dated a friend of Sadie's?"

*I did? Interesting.*

He'd dated a lot of women.

"Did he mention the name of this friend? Or where she lived?"

Dad shook his head. "But I think she was from Port Chance, too."

If he'd dated anyone from Port Chance, it couldn't have lasted very long. Who was this mystery woman

Dad donned his oven mitts as he shrugged. He flipped off the hood of his sweatshirt. The sun had changed positions and peeked from behind the enormous dogwood at the end of the driveway.

"I'll have to ask him about that. I'm drawing a blank."

"How are you handling living with your sister?" Dad asked. "A month is a bit different than a few days."

"We're good so far. I think she's glad I'm there even if we get in each other's way quite a bit. It's a small cabin for a big personality like Cara's."

Dad chuckled. "Amen to that. We'd better get this big boy into the house so it can sit for a bit." He lifted the roasting pan and nodded toward the door. "You'd better clear a path for me inside. This is *hot*."

A half hour later, all twenty-seven of them filled plates at the buffet around the kitchen island before finding seats at the three tables dressed in Thanksgiving finery. After Dad's prayer, they'd go around the tables, saying what they were thankful for.

There was the usual "my health" from Uncle Joe.

The touch of humor from Aunt Gabrielle. "I'm thankful for the ability to run faster than my husband on our hikes so the coyotes get him, not me."

"Blythe's pumpkin pie."

"My dear grandkids."

"I'm thankful the Bears beat the Packers last weekend."

Hayes paused when it was his turn. This heartfelt stuff didn't come naturally to him, but he knew what he wanted to say.

"I'm thankful I'm able to stay with Cara while she recuperates—"

"—from being clumsy," Cara finished. The room erupted in laughter followed by a collective "*awww*." Next to him, Cara playfully bumped his shoulder with hers.

But there was something else that came to mind as he sat with his head bowed, listening to the tradition continue its way around the room. It flitted into his conscience like a bird settling on just the right branch, in no hurry to fly away.

*Sadie.*

# Chapter Nineteen

The Wendell Black Friday shopping tradition took a backseat to helping Janie find her wedding dress on the day after Thanksgiving. Sadie and the other Wendell women met at Coral Lane Bridal in Greenhaven, a brightly lit, white-washed shop which contrasted with the bleakness of the November sky outside. Another late-fall storm brewed in the west.

Excited chatter filled the room as everyone waited for Janie to appear in yet another gown. The wedding was set for next May.

"This one's it," Cora Martin, Janie's soft-spoken friend, said to the rest of them with one hand cupped around her mouth in a mock-whisper. She lounged on a blush velvet settee next to Rose with her stockinged feet tucked under a flowing boho print skirt. "I feel it."

Rose shook her head. "Janie's too hard to please to green-light anything before she tries on at least ten dresses."

"I heard that!" Janie shouted from within the dressing room amid a rustle of satin and tulle.

Mom lifted her mocktail in Rose's direction. "I'm inclined to agree with you."

Cora snorted. "Maybe I met the easy-to-please version of Janie when she lived in Hendricks. I was under the impression she hated shopping."

Cora had come down from Minnesota for the weekend event. While Janie lived in Hendricks for several years, she and Cora, a librarian, had become fast friends. Sadie had met Cora on the woman's first visit to Port Chance since Janie moved back home, and talked with her most recently at Janie's last birthday.

Sadie perched on the edge of a stiff, upholstered side chair, quietly taking in the scene with growing impatience. She itched to get back to the rehab center, but guilt gnawed at her. Of course Janie wanted to share the day of finding the perfect dress with everyone. Sadie wished she bubbled with the same enthusiasm as everyone else in the room, but she couldn't muster the excitement.

Sadie yawned.

Next to her, Rory shifted slightly, saying in a low voice, "Your boredom is showing."

Sadie glanced at Rory. Leave it to her best friend to put Sadie's feelings into words. She'd always been Sadie's conscience personified. As Sadie's oldest and dearest friend, Rory was practically a Wendall, too, so much so that Janie asked Rory to be a bridesmaid. It'd been Rory's recommendation that led them all to this shop in the first place. But Sadie couldn't feel more out of place. Even no-nonsense Kit, wherever she was, had shown more excitement for this appointment than Sadie did when Janie proposed the idea.

"Is it that obvious?" she whispered back.

CHRISTMAS IN PORT CHANCE

"As if it's emblazoned on the front of your shirt," Rory said with a sympathetic smile. She opened her big blue eyes for emphasis. Rory's flare for dressing in statement pieces was offset by her minimalist makeup and fly-away curls. Today she'd secured her shoulder-length tresses into a bun with a tie-dyed silk scarf.

"I'm trying," Sadie said under her breath.

Rory patted Sadie's hand with reassurance. "I know sitting here is tough on you. As happy as you are for Janie and Mark, I'm sure the topic of marriages and weddings still makes you uncomfortable."

"That's putting it lightly."

Yet Hayes's face flashed into her mind more than once this morning. And why did the framed photo on the wall across the room keep drawing her attention? Maybe because the image of the couple dressed in wedding attire, holding hands, and gazing adoringly into each other's eyes reminded her of what marriage was supposed to look like.

Kit breezed into the lounge room seconds later, rapping on the dressing room door as she passed it. From inside, Janie scolded Kit for being late.

"Not too late to catch you saying 'yes' to the dress, right?" Kit shot back with a wink to room. "How many 'noes' did I miss?"

Rose held up three fingers. "I have a good feeling about the next one, though."

Kit plunked down into the empty chair beside Rory. She stretched her legs, crossing them at her ankles. Kit's beat-up work boots earned a scathing look from Mom.

The dressing room door opened. Janie stepped out and twirled. She almost tripped on the cloud of tulle and feathers hiding her lower half. The mermaid-style dress hugged her curves from the waist up, but the skirt was something else. No wonder Janie could barely move.

"What *is* that?" Kit asked.

Janie looked down at herself like she had the same question. "It's not my style, I'll tell you that. I liked it better on the rack."

"Good," said Kit. "I was about to call the zoo to ask if they're missing one of their trumpet swans."

Sadie couldn't hold back her laugh like everyone else. Her youngest sister had a knack for keeping the mood light.

Over the next twenty minutes, Janie modeled three more dresses. Sadie checked the time on her phone while they waited for the next. She listened in as Rory chatted with Kit about the proposed upgrade of the riverfront path next summer. It'd affect both of their businesses as Rory's Blue Door GlassWorks studio sat on the point next to Larkspur State Park, and the state planned to extend the path past her home studio. Rory lamented about how her small parking lot might be overrun with construction equipment, disrupting her peace.

"I'm not very good with change," Rory admitted. "I like my little slice of heaven there. Maybe it'll bring more business with the path being upgraded, but I'm not looking forward to the chaos of construction next summer."

That would be a nightmare for someone like Rory who valued her tranquility. That's why Sadie related so well to Rory. Sadie's own peace of mind had been thrown for a loop this last month with Cara's broken ankle and Hayes's extended stay. But as the days passed, her heartbeat galloped at his sudden appearances around the property, a surprising change from the flashes of annoyance she'd felt in the beginning.

Sadie startled when Janie burst out of the dressing room. Her smile was a sign she'd found her dress.

"This is it!" she said, making a full twirl on the ball of one foot. "What do y'all think?"

The tea-length A-line dress wasn't a conventional wedding dress, but Sadie hadn't expected anything else for her older sister. It had a lace floral overlay that cut up the front and matching lace straps that tied in stiff bows at the top of each shoulder. Like Janie, it was bold and stunning. Sadie, on the other hand, wouldn't be caught dead in it.

Their mom clasped her hands together.

Rose hooted and threw her arms in the air.

Kit gave Janie a thumbs up.

There was a general consensus of "yes!"

"Isn't it a dream?" Kit looked pointedly at her. "That dress was made for Janie to wear."

"It's pretty." She nodded, hoping her smile looked genuine enough. Inside, that old feeling of melancholy tickled a spot near her ribcage. At least she could escape back to the rescue center sooner rather than later.

"What are you doing the rest of the day?" Rory asked as the others stood a short time later, gathering purses and handing empty mocktail cups to the shop attendant. Janie and their mother followed the shop owner to a nearby table where they'd finish the details of ordering.

"The school asked us to do a presentation next week, so I'm putting together a short video to go along with the talk." Sadie slipped on her coat.

Rory's jaw dropped. "Wait, *you're* speaking? To an *audience*?"

"Please," she laughed. "That's why I found Cara. I'm just working behind the scenes."

Rory pressed the back of her hand against her forehead. "Phew. I thought I'd jumped to an alternate reality."

Sadie snorted. "I'd rather walk out of here in one of those dresses than speak to a crowd."

Rory gazed forlornly at Janie's collection of gowns now hanging from a rack on the other side of the room, probably contemplating her own wedding. She'd lost her husband unexpectedly a few years ago.

"I'm glad you came this morning," Sadie whispered to change the subject. "I wasn't sure you'd make it here with it being Thanksgiving weekend."

Rory's face brightened as she turned her back to the dress display.

"I'll open up the studio when I get back there. I'm afraid of selling out before the festival next weekend. Are you coming? My new collection of ornaments will make their debut."

Sadie nodded. The Christmas on the River Festival was her favorite event in town, and supporting her artist friend was something she didn't take lightly.

"I wouldn't miss it."

*Chapter Twenty*

That night, Sadie brewed a mug of peppermint tea and settled onto the couch, bringing it to her lips for the first sip, when someone knocked on her door.

It was late. It couldn't be Cara, venturing out after dark, especially wearing her cast.

"It's me, Hayes" came the voice on the other side of her door like she'd projected her thoughts somehow.

She stopped halfway across the room with dawning horror at her flannel bottoms with a rip in one knee and frayed hems. Running a hand through hair she hadn't combed since that morning, she bypassed the mirrored oak hat stand beside the door.

*Goodness, I might scare him away once he gets a look at me. Wait, so what?*

Oh, but she cared all right. Why else did she question her ratty attire to begin with?

To Hayes's credit, he gave her a once-over when she opened the door, but he didn't grimace or shudder or anything equally disapproving. Instead, he flashed a grin.

"I need sugar. Please."

Her outburst of laughter surprised them both.

"What's so funny?" he asked.

"It's just so...cliché." She stepped aside for him to enter, still giggling to herself.

"Cara sent me. She used all the sugar making her Thanksgiving pie." He shrugged. "Cookies are on her list now. It's for some event she's going to tomorrow. Vague, I know, but it sounds like a do-or-die thing, don't ask me." He stopped babbling. That was more than she'd ever heard him say in one breath.

"No need to explain." She hadn't meant to make him feel self-conscious.

"Is that your tree still in the box?"

Sadie looked over her shoulder as she opened her baking cabinet. "Yes."

Hayes followed her toward the kitchen, but had stopped near the couch, staring at the fireplace.

"But we hauled it in here more than two weeks ago. Why haven't you unpacked it yet?"

She shrugged, pulling down the sugar canister, too tired to offer an explanation, let alone leave out the parts that might invite more questions. She hadn't the energy anymore for that story.

"Let's put it up," he said. "I can help."

"Not necessary. Really."

"But look at all of this. We'll have it up in no time." Hayes pulled open a flap of the ornament box, peeking inside.

While it secretly thrilled her that Hayes wanted to decorate the tree with her, it'd take forever with the number of ornaments her mother had passed on to her and her sisters during the Great Christmas Clean-Out last year. Their mother had decided five Christmas trees in the house were four too many.

Besides, what could she and Hayes talk about for that long? And the tree, it'd be a mess with as little as she'd be able to focus.

"I'm just going to give you this whole canister. Cara can give it back to me tomorrow."

"You're trying to change the subject."

She snorted. "You're the one who came here looking for sugar. Now you want to decorate my tree. I'm not the one going off-topic."

"Let's do it," he prodded.

"I like doing it myself."

*Wasn't this just another version of the same old excuse?*

She'd perfected the art of procrastination where her Christmas decorations were concerned. They'd always been a point of contention with Evan. He couldn't stand the house in disarray as she rearranged furniture and decor for "stuff that you only put out for a month before it goes back into storage for the next eleven months." Sadie bristled at the memory.

Before she said another word, Hayes opened both boxes. Sadie abandoned her task for finding sugar and joined him in the living room to stand by while he lifted the lid.

"Hayes, really."

"What? Are you going to deny me the fun of putting up your tree?"

"But I don't want your help." It sounded harsh, but he wasn't getting the hint.

The tree looked even more pathetic than she imagined. Branches bent at unnatural angles, a confusion of plastic needles and wired boughs. Tangles of light strings were bunched together, too, not even rolled into the tidy balls like how Rose stored hers. She breathed loudly through her nose, drawing Hayes's attention.

"It's not that bad," he said. "It'll be up in no time."

"Lights are usually the death of me." Now that the mess was exposed, maybe getting a little help wouldn't be so bad.

He looked squarely at her, his soft expression melting away a little of her frustration and doubt.

"Tell you what. Why don't you make yourself a cup of tea. I'll get started," he said.

"Tea is already made. I hadn't planned to—"

"Okay, you sit and enjoy your tea. I'll put the tree together while you watch," he insisted.

"This isn't your tree. I feel guilty sitting by while you work."

"Work is waiting on my sister all day long."

She nodded. She liked his decisiveness. Goodness knows she needed that in her life. Her constant waffling about decisions lately, it wasn't like her at all.

"What are you shaking your head about?" Hayes asked.

"My procrastination habits."

"You have a lot on your mind."

It was true, but it felt selfish to acknowledge aloud. Hayes was without a job. Now, he'd taken on the responsibility of caring for Cara, too.

He twisted and reinserted boughs, and untangled a multitude of lights still wound through the branch tips. Talking with him was easy; their conversation flowed without the awkward pauses. She didn't mind the view from where she sat, either. Hayes's broad shoulders almost stretched as wide as the tree itself. The light behind him accentuated his profile—the strong jaw, his artfully disheveled hair, a nose that looked in perfect proportion to the rest of his face. She caught herself sighing when he rolled up his flannel shirt sleeves, exposing sinewy forearms.

*Careful, girlfriend.*

He's the last thing she needed in her life, though she'd found herself contemplating more and more what an easy presence he'd be to have around.

Hayes stepped back to admire his handiwork. He'd taken care of redistributing the lights, which she'd never had the patience for. It didn't look half bad for twenty minutes' worth of work.

"How did you do that?" she asked.

Hayes looked bewildered. "What?"

"Make the lights look so evenly spaced."

He studied the tree. "It must be the engineer in me."

"Whatever it is, you're hired for the rest of my life."

He grinned then did a double-take. His slow grin grew wider. And he was staring at her like...*oh*. Sadie sipped her tea, hiding behind the mug as her face went up in flames.

"I accept," he said.

"The pay isn't that great. Tea and cookies is the best I can offer."

"That doesn't sound like such a bad deal," Hayes said, rubbing his hands together. "Now for the ornaments."

"Oh, I can do that myself." She set her mug on the coffee table, reluctantly coming out of her Hayes-fueled reverie.

He studied her with a slight frown. "It's really no trouble."

"I...thanks, but I'd rather do it. And Cara is waiting for the sugar."

"She has plenty of time to bake," he said hurriedly.

Sadie almost asked if he was telling the truth. Did he even need the sugar to begin with?

Hayes bent over the ornament box.

"Well, lookie at this one." He'd pulled an ornament from the top, dangling the hook between two fingers. "Aren't you a cute little bug."

Smiling, she pushed up from the couch to see which one had drawn his response. A dainty walnut shell ornament she'd made in kindergarten, halved and lined with a cotton ball, was sprinkled with glitter. A cutout of her face—a school photo—was glued to the center of the downy circle. She snickered at the corny nostalgia of it. Hayes hung it on the nearest branch where it swayed and sparkled, catching the lamplight.

"There are more where that one came from." She heaved the box onto the coffee table to save their backs. "One of the Wendell traditions is the annual ornament-making party."

Hayes stopped digging to look at her. His brows lifted. "I'll start looking for my invite," he teased.

"Seriously, it's the only time of year we come to my parents' house with expectations of Christmases past. There have been so many fun memories made on that one day over the years. My friends used to beg to come."

He reached for another ornament, but he slowed as if something came to mind.

"Do many of your friends still live in Port Chance?" he asked as he hung another ornament. "Most of mine have relocated. It seems no one settles in their hometowns for life anymore."

Sadie let out a good-humored huff. "Except me and my sisters."

"I didn't mean that in a negative way. It's just an observation."

"I have a couple of friends who've stuck around town."

She stood on tiptoes to hang a straw star from one of the upper branches.

Hayes reached for the next ornament at the same time Sadie did, and their fingers brushed together. She snatched hers away like she'd been burned, while he froze. His fingers flexed briefly before their gazes locked.

"You first," he murmured.

The lump in her throat couldn't be dislodged. *In fact, it might be growing.*

Sadie plucked the next ornament from the pile. He took another, too. But as his fingers closed around one in particular, Sadie almost grabbed it out of his hand.

*No, no, no.*

It'd been so long since she'd unpacked her ornaments she'd forgotten about it.

With good reason.

Sadie clamped her teeth together, hoping he'd put it on the tree without asking about it. But how could he not with its inscription begging to be explained.

Hayes held up Rory's creation, a gift given to her in happier times.

"What's the story behind this one?"

# Chapter Twenty-One

Hayes's attention snapped to the initials on the front of the ornament as it dangled between them.

*E & S*

The letters were etched into the trunk of a little wooden tree. Copper wire sprung from the top of the trunk to replicate tree branches, and the red and green heart-shaped glass beads on each copper branch tip were its leaves. It was a beautiful ornament. Someone had designed this for Sadie. Maybe the handiwork of "E."

He chanced a look at her when she didn't answer right away, and the mix of emotions playing across her features told him he'd asked the wrong question.

"I'm sorry. Maybe that's too personal to share."

She stood immobilized, gazing down at the felted wool polar bear on skis in her hand. Taking her time to find the perfect spot for it, she reached for the farthest point she could on the tree and affixed the ornament, her fingers nimbly pulling the needles through the yarn loop. Then she faced him with an unwavering look.

"No, it's not," she said softly. "'S' is me, obviously. The 'E' is my ex…ex-husband. Evan."

Hayes almost set the ornament back in the box, but she gently took it from him to place it on a branch herself. Her jaw ticked as she concentrated on the task.

"My friend Rory made it for me…us," she said finally. "It was a Christmas gift the first year after Evan and I married."

He nodded.

"I don't talk about it much." She let out a short laugh. "That period of my life is one I don't like to revisit too often." A shadow of annoyance crossed her face until she regained her composure, then the smile was back.

"Again, I shouldn't have asked. I'm sorry."

"Really. It's fine. Suppressing my emotions doesn't help, I'm told." Her tone was still soft, but now it held an edge of determination.

"But maybe you should get rid of the reminder?" He suddenly felt oddly protective, though he had no right to feel that way.

"It's too gorgeous to toss. I could never get rid of anything Rory made."

Rory. That name rang a distant bell.

The more he turned the name over in his mind, the clearer it became that this must be Sadie's artist friend Randy had mentioned. Fragments of a memory flashed in his mind now.

A woman with wild blonde hair.

A summer music festival.

Sitting outside of a beer tent with Randy. There'd been other people with them.

It'd been at least fifteen years ago. A lot had happened since then. Had he even graduated from college at that point?

He couldn't concentrate, not with Sadie two feet away looking completely huggable in her flannel pajamas and the revelation about the ornament clouding his thoughts.

He'd known of her divorce, thanks to Cara. Also, that her ex had been a real jerk. But that was it. He'd purposely steered clear of anything that might broach the subject with Sadie, but how was he to know an innocent ornament might be a trigger?

"It's okay. I'm better now," she went on. "It took years of talking it out to get to where I am now. Still work to do, though." Her words drifted in and out as he fitted together a mental puzzle, one with missing pieces.

"Huh?" He'd missed something she'd said while buried deep in his own thoughts.

"Evan and I. It was never meant to be, but even during the worst experiences, you grow from them." She resumed hanging ornaments, keeping her focus on the tree. "Do you know what I mean?" She darted a glance his way before she moved behind the tree.

"I guess? I...can't think of a time when—"

Sadie reappeared on the other side of the tree to pluck two more ornaments from the box.

"That's okay," she interrupted. "My sisters say I live inside my own head too much."

*Idiot! Way to NOT commiserate.* If ever he wished for a rewind button for his mouth, this was the time.

"I don't think I'm as introspective as that," he managed to say.

"It's more of a curse sometimes, so count yourself lucky," she said lightly.

*Evan.* Cara had mentioned him. He needed to see a photo of this guy. Something wasn't clicking.

Sadie stood over the box and heaved a sigh. "I have more ornaments than I remember."

His lips twitched as he fought a smile. "Yet you'll make more at your ornament party."

"You should come," she said in a lilting tone. "Cara's invited."

"Me, make ornaments? It'd definitely be a first." It was so not his thing, but oddly enough, it sounded...fun? Sadie actually *wanted* him there.

"That's the point. We eat, make stuff, laugh. It's a good time. No one's ornaments turn out well except for Janie's and Rory's anyway. And my mom's, I guess."

"I don't know..."

"It's sure to rank as your favorite Christmas memory for years to come."

A smile spread across his face. "How can I turn that down?"

His phone vibrated in his back pocket. No sooner had he answered Cara's call than she blurted loudly enough that Sadie heard, too.

He pressed the speaker button. "Hey, Cara. I'm here with Sadie."

"Where's my sugar?"

"Sorry," Sadie said, raising her voice so Cara could hear her. "I roped him into helping me decorate my tree."

Silence.

Sadie exchanged a confused glance with him, but her lips twitched with amusement.

"Oh," Cara said with overdone enthusiasm. Another pause. "Take your time then. Really, no hurry." The connection went dead a second later.

He and Sadie continued to stare until she burst out laughing.

"I have to admit I thought the sugar request was an excuse," she said, ducking her head away from him to rummage in the ornament tub again.

"An excuse? Why would I make that—"

"To come over here."

She lifted her head with a bold stare. Her playful expression dared him to deny it.

With pulse-pounding certainty, Sadie was flirting with him. His roller-coaster mind couldn't think of a way to respond. An hour ago he would have jumped at the chance to toss a little playful banter around, but with the ex talk and Rory revelation, his thoughts were as tangled as that jumble of Christmas lights he'd unwound.

Sadie's eyes widened as the corners of her mouth turned upside down. "What I meant was...was that...oh, never mind. Cara's waiting on that sugar."

"I do have something else to tell you."

She looked at him again with an earnest expression. "Oh?"

"I got that job. The one in Des Moines."

Her hopeful smile didn't falter, but now it looked frozen.

"I'll start the first of the year."

She turned away so abruptly that Hayes thought she hadn't heard him, but she spoke over her shoulder on the way into the kitchen.

"That's great. Congrats," she said as she came back with the whole canister of sugar. She thrust it into his hands before she went back to decorating.

Hayes stared at the top of her head as she dipped into the box, pulling out a handful of ornaments.

"Better hurry or she'll call again. Then you'll really get an earful." There was an underlying waver in her voice. She wouldn't look at him.

"Sadie."

"Thanks for your help," she said brightly. "I've got it from here."

As he walked out into the night toward Cara's cabin, he pored over their latest interaction.

*If there's a chance with that woman, let me not blow it before it's too late.*

Or maybe that time had already come and gone.

# Chapter Twenty-Two

Before noon on Monday, Sadie had just finished cleaning the inside cages when the crunch of gravel outside made her pause. She nodded to herself. *Good timing*.

Prepping this school presentation had kept her mind off of the news that Hayes would leave Port Chance at the end of the month. She still felt the stiffness of her smile and how her heart had dropped into her shoes when he told her.

She'd just gotten used to seeing his truck parked next to Cara's cabin.

And hearing him greet Todd the red fox every morning as he passed the outside enclosures to bring Cara a freshly brewed thermos of coffee.

She didn't mind the musky scent of his cologne either, reminding her of a bonfire and the crispness of wet pine trees after a rain. It overpowered the animal smells of the intake building. No complaints there.

Outside, a door closed.

She pushed aside the curtain, expecting to see Cara parked

outside the building to wait for her. They'd head to the school, make sure the projector synced with her laptop, and get settled inside the gymnasium before the classes filed onto the bleachers. Her heart raced in anticipation of being scrutinized by so many eyes, and she wasn't even giving the presentation. Her only role would be holding Monte with a smile on her face.

Her entire script melted away when Hayes approached the front door, not Cara.

He walked in, all swagger and brushed suede. His coat collar was turned up, accentuating his strong jawline with the softness of the shearling lining. Her heart stuttered to a stop, then thumped wildly to a new rhythm.

"Hey there. How's your day been so far?"

Her throat suddenly felt a little constricted. They hadn't talked since his new job revelation.

"So far, so good. No new intakes. All squirrels accounted for and healthy. No escapees," she said quickly.

He nodded with a grin. "Your Florence Nightingale ways prevail."

Sadie closed the box where she stored prescription medication, then shoved it into the cabinet behind her. She busied herself with her back turned until she pulled it together. Embarrassment from her attempt to tease him the other night still stung, too. Her blood pounded in her temples as her words came back to haunt her.

*...an excuse to come over here.*

How stupid was that to say? Serves her right to feel mortified. No wonder he took the opportunity then to tell her he'd be leaving Port Chance.

Hayes cleared his throat. "So, I'm here because Cara said

she's running late getting her X-rays. She'll meet us at the school."

She gasped and grabbed her phone off the examination table.

"Cara didn't tell me that." She hadn't called *or* texted with this news.

"She didn't want to worry you. It's fine. We'll take everything you need, and like I said, she'll meet us there. Maybe she'll even beat us."

"Is she at least driving? Or is she still stuck at the hospital?" She couldn't cancel this presentation. Donations had already started trickling in since the Killeens proposed the fundraiser to the PTO. If she had to delay this, it wouldn't look good. The center desperately needed the help.

He came around the table to rest his hands on her shoulders, dipping his head so they could see eye to eye.

"We've got this, Sadie. Don't worry. She'll be there." His eyes penetrated hers. She tried to ignore the ripple of delight flowing through each arm, but the sensation overpowered her nervous energy, at least for the moment.

"What can I grab?" he asked, releasing her shoulders to rub his hands together, glancing around the room.

That spurred her to action.

Laptop. Projector. Bag filled with swag for the classroom teachers. She'd grab Monte's cage.

"I can get that," Hayes offered, eyeing Sadie as she lifted Monte's bulky travel carrier.

"He gets stressed if anyone but me carries his cage."

"Cara, too?" He opened the door for her as they made their way to his truck.

"Yep, I can't explain it."

"And he's the best ambassador for this kind of thing?"

Sadie set the carrier snugly on the backseat. "A perfect angel. He loves a crowd. The bigger, the better."

Soon they were on their way, winding through the back roads outside Port Chance toward Sycamore Elementary. Outside her window, the barren farm fields rolled by dotted with patches of unmelted snow. A flock of turkeys congregated near a dilapidated barn, scavenging for leftover harvest corn. The hasty way she'd dismissed him the other night weighed on her now, like it had off and on the last few days.

"I really am happy for you, by the way. About the Des Moines job."

He glanced over with a quick smile, studying her like he didn't believe her. "Thank you. It was hard to pass up," he said finally as his attention returned to the road.

"Cara says she'll never see you now, though." She coughed to get rid of the hitch in her voice.

Hayes tossed his head back with a laugh. "By the time I leave here at the end of the month, she'll be anxious for a break."

"Were you two close growing up?"

"Yeah, we were. Our brother is five years older, so even though we were all pretty tight, Cara and I are closer in age. She was always a little rough and tumble, too, so she didn't mind tagging along with my friends and me." He snapped the lid off his fountain drink to catch a mouthful of ice.

"She's a lot like my sister Kit. Maybe that's why I like her. She's no-nonsense without the usual sisterly conflicts."

Hayes chuckled again, a pleasant, throaty sound.

He had no clue how charming he was. It was impossible to pretend her nerves didn't crackle when he was around. His teeth flashed. She pulled her attention away lest he catch her staring.

"I'll be back to visit more," he continued as he crunched on more ice. "I can't see myself putting in the hours I did at the last place. This company promotes a family-first message, they say." He lifted his brows. "We'll see."

"I'm sure Cara will love that."

He glanced at her again. "Any time you need a hand here... I'd be happy to help. Des Moines isn't that far away."

A lump rose in her throat. His willingness to jump in more than once since she'd met him, it meant the world to her. His mere presence was like a balm. She found herself thinking about him when she prepped meals for the animals, when she drove into town, and especially when she lay in bed at night, sometimes foregoing reading to turn off the lights and let her mind wander.

How would it feel if he took her hand? Would his skin be soft and warm like she imagined?

Or if they kissed, would his lips feel like a whisper or more forceful like he'd been waiting his whole life for Sadie?

She let out a sigh, which came out more loudly than she intended. Her anxiety about this presentation made her more emotional than usual.

"It'll be all right," he said softly. "I've got your back today."

All she could do was keep watching the passing landscape and nod or he'd see that her eyes had started to water.

## Chapter Twenty-Three

Sadie's worried frown greeted Hayes when he hurried into the school after dropping her and Monte off at the front door and parking the truck.

"Have you checked your phone messages? Has Cara left the hospital yet?" Sadie said after the office assistant buzzed him into the vestibule. "She didn't even answer my text."

"She's either in the X-ray room or she's driving," he said, grabbing the projector and the rest of the gear. They followed the office assistant down a long hallway toward the gym. "Cara never texts when she drives."

As they walked, Sadie brushed the snowflakes still clinging to his coat. He nodded to the Christmas tree set up by the office as they passed it, but Sadie didn't seem to register that it was a giving tree for the shelter. It was simple but charming. Pinecones had been transformed into foxes, raccoons, rabbits, and opossums by the students. Wrapped gifts covered the floor underneath the tree, all designated for Furever Friends. Sadie kept her eyes on the floor in stony silence as they were led down the hall.

She glanced at him when he chuckled at the animal drawings taped to the walls on either side of them.

"I can't believe you find this funny," Sadie said. "I'm on the verge of a heart attack, and you're smiling like a puppet master is tugging at the corners of your mouth." She pulled an imaginary string near her mouth with her free hand and forced a grin.

"I'm sorry. It will all work—"

"You don't understand. Talking comes naturally to Cara. Even with a prepared speech, I can't get the words out."

They reached for their pockets when someone's phone buzzed. It was Sadie's. She muttered, "Please, please, please," under her breath before she answered. At the same time, the office assistant stopped inside the gym near the bleachers, motioning to Sadie where she could set up.

"I'll take care of everything from here," he assured the woman who then left to get back to the office.

"How close are you?" Sadie said into the phone.

Hayes read her eyebrows since he only heard half of their conversation. They were hopefully arched one second and distressed slashes the next.

"What'll I do if you don't get here on time? We can't cancel."

Cara must have responded with something that set Sadie's mind at ease, at least temporarily. She nodded decisively before telling Cara to be careful.

"Well?"

Sadie hugged her arms against her chest. "She says she'll make it, but there's an accident on the I-80 bridge."

"Come sit." He led her to the bottom row of bleachers. "I have a temporary solution."

She sank onto the bench while he fetched one of the plastic bags she'd stashed in the outside pocket of her duffel. He filled it with the rest of the ice from his drink cup, looped the top closed with a knot, and sat next to her.

"Lift your hair from your neck," he said.

Her eyes flitted from his face to the floor and back to him as she gathered her hair, twisting it into a knot while holding it against the back of her head.

"What are you doing?" she asked with a crooked smile.

"Icing your vagus nerve."

"My what?" she asked, her eyes widening with alarm.

"Cooling the back of your neck stimulates your vagus nerve which, in turn, can relieve stress."

"How do you know this?" There was a lightness in her tone.

*Good, it's already worked and I haven't even applied the bag yet.*

"One of my college roommates studied physical therapy."

She cringed, closing her eyes when he pressed the bag on her neck. Sadie held her shoulders tight against the cold shock, but as the seconds ticked by, they slowly dropped as she relaxed.

"How much time do we have before the kids come in?" she asked in a dreamy voice. Her eyes were still shut.

He checked his watch. "About ten minutes."

"How's Monte doing?" She almost slurred her words.

Beside her, Monte lay on his side in his cage, his underbelly exposed with contentment. His little black opossum nose twitched when Sadie said his name, and he opened one lazy eye to regard Hayes with indifference.

"Pretty chill, like you."

She huffed with a smile. Her neck rolled a little, exposing

149

the skin above her collar. Hayes couldn't take his eyes off the spot.

"I may look chill, but my insides are bubbling like a soup pot." She opened her eyes to peer into Monte's cage. "If I left his side right now, he'd pace the perimeter of this carrier. His teeth click together when he's nervous, too. And when he's really stressed, he screeches."

"That will liven up the presentation," he croaked. He imagined how that spot would feel underneath his lips, his nose buried in her hair. Even sitting an arm's length away, the breezy peach and floral notes of whatever scent she wore was electrifying. It reminded him of summer at his parents' Michigan beach house. He'd go over the edge if he inhaled it up close.

"That's not going to happen since Cara will get here on time, and I'll keep Monte company. Right?" She opened one eye when he didn't answer right away.

"If she said she'll be here, she'll be here." Sadie's ongoing commentary about Cara's absence was starting to make *him* nervous.

"Let's get the projector set up." Sadie scooted away from him to click open the equipment case. "If I sit here any longer, I'll be a pool of jelly."

They scrambled to erect the portable screen and get the projector ready, working quietly but efficiently until everything was in the proper place. Sadie projected the opening slide onto the screen when the first class shuffled into the gym. She glanced up, froze, then caught his eye. Her panic-stricken face grew pale, which made him pause.

Sadie looked helpless and alone.

He'd seen this look once before. Murky fragments of a

memory floated around in his mind, each part opposing the others like oil and water.

Hayes rubbed his forehead.

*Why can't I piece it together?*

## Chapter Twenty-Four

S adie's middle felt like a butterfly hatchery. Worse yet, her voice kept cracking as if she'd swallowed glass. She guzzled half her water bottle, hoping it was that simple, then checked her phone for a message from Cara yet again. Nothing.

"You're going to float away if you drink any more of that," Hayes said.

"I can't—" she croaked. Another drink. "Can't talk. How will this even work?" She tossed the bottle onto her bag on the floor and slipped her hastily jotted notes from her back pocket. "Have you heard from Cara?"

Hayes checked his phone. "Nope."

"I can't do this. I didn't get a chance to prep. Cara can wing something like this on a minute's notice. Not me."

He took her by the shoulders and looked at her with an intensity that made Sadie shudder.

"You know the whole imagine-the-crowd-in-their-under-wear trick?

She nodded. *Seriously*?

He wrinkled his nose. "Doesn't work."

"That's helpful."

"Try this instead: pretend you're talking to your most-trusted person. The one who makes you feel completely at ease."

"But there will be two hundred fifty sets of eyeballs on me."

"Doesn't matter. Have a conversation with that one person in mind. How would you talk to him or her if it were the two of you?"

She nodded again, peering over his shoulder toward the door as the last class filed onto the bleachers, her mind whirling. One of the teachers shut the door, a signal it was almost time to start.

*Relax your shoulders.*

She grabbed her water again, took another drink, then screwed on the top, twisting it rhythmically back and forth, thinking.

The intake building was her safe haven. It comforted her knowing she eased her animal patients' suffering. She often talked to them because she believed it contributed to their healing.

But they weren't people. Her life wasn't a Cinderella story, with talking animals as her only companions.

"Okay." It wasn't very convincing, but at least her voice stayed steady this time.

The principal walked up to the wooden podium facing the bleachers. She tapped the mic with her finger as a *whump, whump* sounded through the room. A deafening hush came over the young audience. Sadie was certain they could hear her heart pounding against the walls of her chest.

"Boys and girls. We have a special treat for you today. Some of you may know Ms. Wendell who runs Furever Friends Wildlife Rehabilitation in Port Chance. She's here with us—"

Her stomach danced frantically. She couldn't see clearly as her eyes clouded with tears. Not only would she make a fool of herself in front of children, but Hayes would witness the moment. Beside her, he stepped closer. His hand closed over hers.

"You've got this. I'm right here."

His hand was warm and all-encompassing. She wished his reassurance erased the terror coursing through her. If only she could turn his words over in her mind at leisure, especially the 'I'm right here' part. After this nightmare ended, those three words deserved a little more attention.

Principal Lindquist continued her introduction, drawing Sadie's attention again as if someone had turned up the volume on the sound system. The woman's voice was back, blaring full force, echoing inside her mind.

"—so if you'd give a warm welcome to Ms. Sadie Wendell, she's going to tell you about the rescue and the patients that come under her care."

Her feet were bricks as she walked toward the microphone, weighing her down, slowing her movements. She slipped the hastily written outline from her pocket again and smoothed the wrinkles from the paper as she fought to decipher the notes that now didn't make sense.

"Hi there, boys and girls. Thank you for allowing me to come to your school today. I've been looking..."

Her voice cracked. She cleared it, glancing at Hayes. He nodded encouragingly.

"...forward to this all month. I'm a little nervous so if you hear me start squeaking or making barking noises in my throat, I promise you I'm not turning into one of my patients."

Some kids laughed. A boy shouted, "That would be sooo funny!" before an adult popped up to sit next to him.

Smiling, Sadie looked down at her outline even though the letters blurred. The pause allowed her to gather her bearings again.

"I'm a licensed wildlife rehabilitation specialist. That means I try to make sick and hurt wild animals well again. Then, hopefully, they get to live back in the wild where they belong."

When her head started swimming, she filled her lungs with a cleansing breath. *It'll be okay.*

"I'm going to talk a little about what a typical day looks like at my wildlife center, Furever Friends Wildlife Rescue, then I'll take questions."

It helped to look at a distant spot near the top of the bleachers where no one sat as she spoke. Her focus shifted between that neutral point and Hayes. He stood near the far door with his arms crossed, the only man in the room, his gaze never wavering from her. The notion of Hayes in the audience had terrified her minutes ago, but her fear gave way to comfort.

*Thank goodness he's here.*

\* \* \*

Two teachers followed the last class as they exited the gymnasium forty-five minutes later. Hayes handed one of them the stickers and bookmarks Sadie had brought along for each class. Sadie held onto Monte, who'd tucked his nose into the crook of her arm, so everyone could get a close look at the opossum.

"You'll have all the volunteers you need in about ten years," one of the teachers joked. "A very enlightening presentation. I know the kids loved it."

"Thank you. That's good to hear."

She and Hayes watched the door close, and the gym became an echo chamber of silence again. She covered her face with one hand.

"I have no idea how I survived that. Have you heard from Cara?"

Hayes nodded. "When she finally got through the accident site, your presentation was half over. She said she'd stop at Bryson's to pick up the supplies order and meet us at home."

Sadie nuzzled Monte's head. The opossum made a soft, churring sound.

"You're stronger than you think," Hayes murmured.

She gazed up at him as an overwhelming sense of gratitude swelled within her. Her plan to avoid him after the other night was temporarily delayed.

"Thanks for being here. I really mean that." His brows knitted together like her words made him uncomfortable, but she had to say this. "I never thought I'd get through that without running out of the room in tears."

Hayes's lips were pressed together in a thin line. He studied the floor.

She chuckled nervously. "You're too quiet. Say something."

"I'm just thinking of another time...when..." He let out a breath, shaking his head as if trying to erase a bad memory.

"What is it?"

His phone dinged with a message then. Hayes seemed relieved. "From Cara again," he said. He read her message aloud. "Let's meet at Café Bonita to celebrate Sadie's milestone."

"I can't. Not after this." A noisy restaurant was the last place she wanted to gather. She needed to go home to recharge from this afternoon by way of a hot tea and a warm bath. A little classical piano music playing in the background wouldn't hurt either. "Tell her I'll take a raincheck, though."

Hayes nodded as he shrugged on his coat. He gathered the rest of her equipment while she helped Monte scramble back into the safe confines of his carrier. They stopped by the office so Sadie could sign out on the clipboard.

Outside, the sky was a thick, gray blanket. The snow had stopped but tiny ice pellets now stung Sadie's cheeks.

"You know, I'll miss it around here when I leave," Hayes said as they made their way to his truck." He shot her a quick look, but Sadie pretended not to notice. "Life seems a lot more exciting in Port Chance than everywhere else."

"Maybe you're hanging out with the wrong people."

Hayes slowed as he approached the driver's side, but Sadie kept going, waiting until he unlocked the truck so she could load Monte onto the backseat. When that didn't happen she peered through the back window, trying to see what took Hayes so long.

He had his head bowed, with both hands planted against the door like he was winded. Hayes blew the air from his cheeks and looked up through the window too, so Sadie quickly turned her head.

*What's he doing?*

She jumped when he suddenly appeared on her side.

"Sadie, I need to tell you something."

"What is it?" The look on his face told her it was serious,

more serious than she needed at the moment, standing in the cold, holding Monte's carrier. Her back started to cramp. She wanted to get home to unwind.

"We've known each other for a while," he said in a measured tone.

"I know. Six weeks, to be exact—" He shook his head before she even finished, so she bit down on her lip. Her patience wasn't exactly filled to the brim now. It'd been depleted as soon as she heard Cara would be late.

"What I'm trying to say is..." He looked down at his boots, still shaking his head.

"We've spent a lot of time together so you feel like you've known me for much longer. I get it." She lifted Monte's cage. "This thing is heavy. Do you mind unlocking the door, please?"

He startled. "Of course."

Sadie cooed to Monte as she set him on the seat, then she climbed into the truck, too. Whatever Hayes tried to tell her made the hair stand up on the back of her neck. She rested her head against the headrest and closed her eyes as the possibilities bounced around in her mind like ping pong balls. She didn't want to hear anything that would test her resolve. Hayes was leaving soon.

*Better to cut my losses now than hope for something that was never meant to be in the first place.*

Hayes climbed into the truck. She felt him looking at her. If she kept her eyes shut, maybe he'd forget all about what he'd been trying to say and take her home.

When the truck engine roared to life, Sadie said a silent prayer of thanks. Whatever was on Hayes's mind could wait until she'd had a good night's sleep. But with luck, he'd forget.

It was easier that way.

# Chapter Twenty-Five

The week passed in a blur. Hayes drove Cara to a farm outside of Port Chance to pick up a load of fresh hay bales someone wanted to donate. He also dug up the troublesome pavers in the walkway that Cara had tripped on, since the ground wasn't yet frozen, and replaced them in a fresh layer of sand.

Sadie avoided him.

Each time he walked into the intake building, she busied herself with some new task, rushing about like he was invisible and she was on a timer. When he asked her yet another inane question, growing more desperate to spark some conversation, her answers grew exponentially shorter.

He waited until Sadie's lunch break rolled around on Wednesday, when she usually retreated to her cabin for a half hour, to ask Cara for her take on Sadie's mood.

"I have no idea. She's been quieter than usual this week," Cara said as she chopped apples for the late-afternoon feedings. "Maybe she's worried about finances. I'm not in the loop about such things. She takes care of the books."

"What about the school fundraiser?"

"I think it's ongoing until Christmas break. Sadie did say that more money usually rolls in this month as people look to increase charitable donations before the end of the year." She finished slicing one apple and took another from the basket. "But I'm wondering if things are slow this year. The economy and all."

Hayes leaned over the counter, resting on his elbows.

"She's a hard one to read most of the time," Cara added. "But she's also pretty open if you ask the right questions."

A little chuckle escaped him. "How am I supposed to know the right questions?"

Cara gave him a side-eye, smiling. "Maybe change topics."

"I've tried."

"What do you mean?"

Hayes told her about the night they'd decorated Sadie's tree together, how she'd opened up a little about her marriage. He'd felt like it was his chance to delve a little deeper into how she'd recovered from Evan and what she wanted for her future, but he'd missed the opportunity for questions. He didn't mention that he'd been hung up on piecing together his shared history with Sadie at the time—a major distraction. He hadn't been thinking straight. But what did that matter anymore? Cara would ask more questions than he had answers for if she found out he'd run into Sadie in the past.

He shook the bowl of apple chunks to watch them settle as Cara added more.

Cara stopped cutting. "You'll be in Des Moines at the first of the year anyway. Long-distance relationships are hard."

"So you're telling me to leave her alone?"

His sister lifted a shoulder. "I'm not saying that. I think you and Sadie are a lot alike. But, you've been here almost two months. If she were interested, you'd know it."

Hayes wasn't sure if he agreed, sometimes thinking there was more happening below the surface with Sadie than she let on. He'd caught her watching him. The night they decorated her tree had held promise if he hadn't ruined it with his relocation news. He almost let out a laugh. Too many *ifs* didn't make a very solid foundation for a relationship.

He focused on the muted reflection of the overhead lights shining on the stainless countertop in front of him. Cara was right. He'd leave Port Chance in a few weeks, so running into Sadie after the new year wouldn't be a given unless he visited Cara. But the more he'd come to know her, the more he wished Des Moines wasn't his destination. Given the two choices, maybe he should have taken the Muscatine job.

If Sadie would've shown even an inkling of interest, choosing one location over the other was a risk he'd have taken in a heartbeat.

# Chapter Twenty-Six

Downtown Port Chance had come alive with the sights, sounds, and scents of Christmas a few days later. Sadie loved everything about this weekend. Even the worst years of her marriage had never diminished her excitement for the Christmas on the River Festival.

Overhead, string lights stretched across the street from lamp post to lamp post, illuminating the tops of the white tents where two dozen artisans displayed their pottery, framed prints, and handcrafted ornaments. The trunks of the trees lining Water Street had been draped in red and white lights so they resembled candy canes. At the end of the street, a handful of food trucks sold hot beverages, cinnamon-dusted kringles, and Bavarian pretzels to the revelers. Sadie, along with Cara and Hayes, walked between the booths, soaking up the festive atmosphere. Calliope music, playing "Have a Holly Jolly Christmas," cut through the conversations and laughter of people standing shoulder to shoulder in the frosty December air.

"Isn't this amazing? It's like a movie set," Cara said. "Thanks for talking me into coming."

"I'm glad you came." Sadie knew Cara would love it, even if she had to hobble down the street in her walking cast.

"Thanks for inviting...us," Hayes added.

Hayes had kept a low profile since she and Cara piled into his truck earlier that night. Sadie kept checking over her shoulder to see if he'd stopped at one of the booths since he was uncharacteristically silent as he followed them through the crowd. Sadie didn't mind. On the contrary, it was better that he wasn't his usual distracting self.

"Isn't this more fun than painting your bathroom?" Sadie asked, pausing to feel the texture of some alpaca scarves draped over a rack. "What was the hard deadline about anyway?"

"I started painting before the ankle incident, then everything ground to a halt. I figured once I was able to walk on the cast without crutches, I'd finish" She shook her head. "Nope. But then Hayes stepped up. Thank goodness it'll be finished before the surgery."

*Of course, Mr. Reliable came through once again.* Had he ever let anyone down in his life?

Cara gritted her teeth with a look toward Hayes. "I'm still not comfortable trusting you with a paint brush in Sadie's cabin, though."

"It's *your* cabin. How many times do I have to say that?" She checked the price tag on one of the scarves.

"I don't own it," Cara countered.

"No, but if you want to paint the bathroom, you're doing me a favor." She pictured Hayes balancing on a ladder wearing a paint-spattered shirt and a bandana tied around his neck, but then she pushed the image out of her mind before it went any farther. It'd probably take Hayes leaving town for good before the intermittent thoughts of him stopped jumping into her mind like popcorn.

Hayes treated them to potato-and-cheese pierogies, and they continued walking amongst the booths as they nibbled on the steaming mini dumplings. Cara stopped to buy hand-carved Santa ornaments from a woodworker's booth for their young nieces. Hayes chose fleece sweatshirts for the girls from another booth. Sadie was in the middle of shopping for a door wreath when her mother's voice startled her.

"I hope that's not for me," Mom said in a muffled tone. "You know I like surprises."

Sadie chuckled as she glanced over her shoulder. Her mother's rosy cheeks peeked out from above a tartan scarf.

"That'll teach you for sneaking up on me. I'm looking for something for the shelter's door. Nothing is catching my eye, though. Did you come alone?"

"Rose and Jordan are here somewhere with the kids," Mom said. "We're meeting back at Santa's house in about ten minutes for photos."

Cara and Hayes rejoined them, shopping bags in hand.

"It's nice to see you again, Hayes," Mom said. "Are you staying through Christmas?"

"That's the plan. Cara's surgery is on Wednesday," he said. "I'll stay with her for the first week."

"There's no sense in you and Cara eating alone on the holiday. We'd love to have you join us for Christmas dinner," Mom offered. "Sadie, don't you think so?"

Sadie barely registered her mother's proposal and imagined

the uncomfortable scenarios before Cara jumped in to nix the idea.

"That's so nice of you, but I'll probably hunker down at home with Christmas so close after my surgery," Cara said.

Relief flooded through her, but it was short-lived.

Cara nudged her brother. "But, Hayes, you should definitely go."

Hayes's attention bounced back and forth between Sadie's mother and Cara before he fixed his sister with a loaded look. He opened his mouth to say something but bit his lip instead.

"Right?" Cara gripped his arm, giving it a little shake to prompt an answer. "Seriously. Don't worry about me."

"I'm not leaving you on Christmas," he said flatly.

"Why not? One of us should enjoy the holiday."

"Let's play it by ear, then," Mom said to Hayes. "I don't want to push you, but maybe you'll be up for coming when all is said and done. If not, I'd love to at least bring you both a meal."

Sadie found herself nodding in agreement. "That's probably a better option."

Part of her hated the idea of Cara and Hayes alone in her cabin on Christmas. With their parents traveling for the holiday, another option to celebrate with family didn't exist. But Hayes and her sisters under one roof was unthinkable. Who knew what embarrassing hijinks Kit and Rose were capable of.

Hayes's chest expanded with a deep breath as their attention shifted to him again. He wore that put-on-the-spot expression Sadie had seen only once—when she'd flirted with him the night they'd decorated her tree. Sadie's face still burned remembering how uncomfortable he'd looked. She bet Hayes couldn't wait until Port Chance disappeared in his rearview mirror in two weeks.

Cara wouldn't let the idea rest, though, and turned to Sadie with a pleading look.

"Can you please insist he come for Christmas dinner?" Cara begged. "If there's anyone here he can't say 'no' to, it's you."

## Chapter Twenty-Seven

Cara was so wrong, but Hayes couldn't call her out on it, not with three sets of eyes on him. He'd lost track of the number of times Sadie turned him down for one reason or another, so he'd officially resigned himself to stop asking, period. Asking him to come for her family's Christmas dinner was as unlikely as Cara following her hospital discharge orders to the letter.

Besides, he'd rather suffer through a dinner with Sadie's stink-eye boring into him from across the table than face his sister's wrath from now into eternity for not going to the Wendells' house.

*You'd better say no. I don't want you infiltrating my family's Christmas.*

He could almost hear Sadie's voice in his head. She didn't have to be vocal to get her point across. A quirk of a brow. The firm set of her lips. He's gotten pretty good at reading her body language.

Cara nudged him more forcefully with her elbow this time.

"I'll save Sadie the trouble of begging me. I'll come to dinner," he blurted.

Cara's and Sadie's jaws dropped, but for different reasons.

"Thank goodness," Cara said.

Sadie's mouth snapped shut. Judging by her stony expression, Sadie might serve his head on a platter instead of the Christmas ham.

Sonya's grin broadened. "Good, it's settled then. And no, you don't need to bring anything. Just yourself."

Cara's expression brightened. "Thanks so much for the offer, Sonya."

"My pleasure, honey. I hope your surgery goes well." Sonya hugged Cara, then shook a finger at him. "Five o'clock dinner, but come at four. Aaron will make you one of his pomegranate fizzes. You'll need it when the Wendell girls come together."

Sonya said goodbye and wandered back into the crowd, leaving Hayes to wonder how he'd found himself with a dinner invitation and no desire to go.

Cara held up a holiday arrangement in the nearest booth. "You'll need to bring a hostess gift."

Beside him, Sadie remained grim-faced until she spotted something up ahead.

"I'll be over there," she said, then promptly left.

"Thanks a lot," he said when Sadie was out of earshot, pulling out his wallet to pay for the arrangement. They waited for the vendor to wrap it. "Sadie would have spoken up if she wanted me there. I'm just a Scroogey intruder."

"Don't be silly," Cara said, continuing to walk after he claimed his purchase. "There'll be enough people at that party anyway if she's set on avoiding you."

"Are you sure you won't be able to come?"

He took little comfort in the fact that Sadie was the only Wendell woman who didn't enjoy his company.

Cara pulled a frown. "I'm positive. I have a date with the couch and AMC. It'll be my last chance to watch *It's a Wonderful Life* for a full eleven months."

Ahead, Sadie had stopped at a booth with glass ornaments dangling from primitive wooden trees. She chatted and laughed with someone inside the tent. He loved seeing her happy. Her sweet smile didn't appear very often, but when it did it looked like the sun breaking through the stormiest sky. Everything about her sparkled at that moment, like her whole being was wrapped in Christmas lights and set aglow. It was almost too much, knowing his time in town was coming to a close.

Cara stopped at the end of a long line stretching in front of a gourmet hot chocolate booth.

"I'm grabbing a drink," she said. "Why don't you join Sadie, and I'll catch up with you."

He slipped a twenty-dollar bill out of his wallet.

"Can you get one for Sadie and me, too? My treat."

He left Cara to join Sadie at the glass booth, checking his phone messages on his walk over. Some paperwork from the Des Moines plant hadn't made it to his inbox yet despite the HR person assuring him it'd come by the end of the day. He hoped to take care of it before Cara's surgery in Iowa City.

"And I told her I'd be happy to take the fox, but I just don't have the time to set up an extensive network of traps," Sadie said to whomever was inside the tent. She glanced at him as he approached. "They'll have to call the trapping guy I work with, but this person doesn't want to spend the money."

"Some people are so entitled," the woman said.

Hayes looked up to match the voice with a face and immediately stopped in his tracks.

*It's her.*

The woman with wild blonde hair narrowed her eyes at him in recognition.

"This is Cara's brother, Hayes Kelley," Sadie said, pulling him by the coat sleeve forward into the glassmaker's booth. "Hayes, this is my good friend, Rory."

He smiled, but his insides withered. Seeing the two women together triggered the memory. It all came back to him in bursts of clarity.

Rory, Randy, Sadie, and Sadie's slimy ex, Evan.

He blinked as Rory continued to stare. He could almost see inside her mind, the gears clicking into place.

They'd all met at a place on the river, a triple date that Randy had arranged. Randy had been dating someone else at the time, a woman Evan couldn't keep his eyes off of which had made everyone in the group uncomfortable, especially Sadie. The guy had spent the entire time hitting on Randy's date, throwing compliments her way, even buying her a second beer when Randy stepped away. Beside him, Sadie sat quietly, shell-shocked and hanging on Evan's every word when he bothered to speak to her. But it was clear she was crushed by his attentiveness to another woman and the lack of respect for his own wife.

Selfless, kind Sadie hadn't deserved that. He'd stayed close to her for the rest of the night, trying to engage her, to help minimize her embarrassment, but doubted he'd had any impact. She and Evan had slipped away at some point. In the meantime, his date—this woman— had understandably been less than impressed with Hayes's attentiveness to Sadie. It was a hot mess of a night. No wonder he'd forgotten the details.

Rory cleared her throat, shooting Sadie a glance before her attention settled on him again. She smiled politely, but the sharpness of her gaze told him she recognized him, too.

"Nice to meet you," Rory said. "Again."

# Chapter Twenty-Eight

Sadie puzzled over how Hayes and Rory already knew each other. She was about to ask this before Cara shoved a hot chocolate into her hand, spilling most of it onto her pants.

"Watch where you're going!" Cara shouted to the retreating backs of two teens jogging through the crowded street. She turned back to Sadie and gasped at her chocolate-streaked white cords. "I'm so sorry! What a mess!"

Hayes took in the damages. "Are you okay?"

Sadie swiped at her stained pants to no avail. The skin on her thighs stung from the hot liquid. "I think so?"

"I'll find some napkins," Hayes said hurriedly, disappearing in the throng of people surrounding them.

Rory offered a handful of napkins from her bag, but it was no use. The almost-full cup of cocoa had run down her legs, pooling into her ankle boots too. She hoped they weren't ruined.

"I have an extra pair of pants at the studio," Rory said, gritting her teeth as she studied Sadie's predicament. "They're work pants, but they might fit."

Sadie shook her head. Soon the fabric would cool and she'd feel the full brunt of the December air.

"I'd better go home to change."

Cara glanced around, irritated. "Hayes will be back any second with napkins. Where is he?"

"I need more than just a few napkins, but tell him thanks anyway." She pulled the fabric away from her skin, which gave her little relief.

"Are you sure?" Rory asked. "You'll come back, won't you? You haven't made it to the gluhwein booth yet. What will you do without this year's commemorative boot mug?"

Sadie chuckled. "I'll survive."

"I'll get you one," Cara said. "This is my fault anyway. I owe you."

Luckily, her mother was where she said she'd be, watching Rose's boys get their annual photo taken with Santa. When Sadie walked up to where her mother waited outside of the white picket fencing surrounding Santa's North Pole display, Sadie couldn't contain her smile. Rose's six-year-old twins were more into the experience than poor Travis. Her teenaged nephew was living his worst nightmare, judging by his scowl and limp posture.

"What happened to you?" Mom said with a sweeping glance at her chocolate-stained pants.

"A full cup of hot chocolate ran into me. Can I use your car to get home?" Her pants were growing stiffer and frostier by the second.

Mom fished her keys out of her coat pocket. "I knew there was a reason I insisted on meeting Rose here."

"You're a lifesaver." She held out her hand for the keys, but Mom withdrew them and cracked a grin.

"Where's Hayes when you need him?" she said.

"He didn't offer, and I didn't ask." She wiggled her fingers for the keys, but Mom held onto them like they were part of a conditional offer.

"That's not very chivalrous."

"In his defense, I didn't give him a chance to offer." *In his defense? Why do I need to cover for him?*

"I'm glad he decided to come for dinner," She handed over the keys. "I hope he won't feel too awkward without his sister."

"Hayes is perfectly comfortable in any situation." This was true. She'd seen him in action, from talking with people who showed up to the rescue unannounced to most recently with the office staff at Sycamore Elementary. His confidence was contagious, too. She still couldn't believe she made it through that afternoon alive.

Mom turned back to her grandsons as they left Santa. Travis couldn't scurry away fast enough.

"I like him. It's too bad he isn't sticking around town. He'd be good for—"

Sadie kissed her on the cheek to stifle her mother's next word.

"Goodnight, Mom. Thanks for the keys."

She hurried away, ruffling Travis's and the twins' heads as she passed them, already dreading the thought of suffering through Christmas dinner with Hayes in the same room. A special plea to keep Kit's and Rose's not-so-discreet comments on the lowdown was in order. She'd enlist Janie for backup.

As Sadie slipped behind the wheel of her mother's car in the next block, she glanced toward the glow of the festival rising above the rooftops of the buildings between her and Water Street. Hayes most definitely had rejoined his sister at Rory's booth by now. An ache crept into her chest for missing out. But as she sat there, the niggling pang had less to do with wishing her night hadn't been cut short by a hot chocolate mishap.

A more insistent thought surfaced once again, this time a shout rather than a whisper.

She didn't want Hayes to leave Port Chance.

# Chapter Twenty-Nine

C hristmas shopping had always added an extra level of stress to Sadie's life during the holidays. She tended to overthink gifts and overspend. As a result, she pushed shopping until the last minute, which resulted in a mad rush of online ordering and navigating long lines of cranky shoppers.

Rory's Blue Door Glass Studio was the exception.

Her friend's shop was like stepping into a rainbow. Simply standing amongst the stained-glass panels, hand-blown hummingbird feeders, and Christmas tree bulbs delighted Sadie. The atmosphere was as peaceful as she could imagine outside the boundaries of Furever Friends.

"Who are you shopping for today?" Rory asked when she met Sadie at the door two days after the festival. Her face shield sat on top of her head, which meant she'd been fusing glass in the workroom before she opened the studio. Rory untied her heavy apron and stored both pieces of equipment behind the counter as Sadie followed her through the store. "I think your dad already bought your mom the limited-edition ornament."

"I didn't come for my family. I'm hoping to find something for Cara." She glanced around at the shelves lining the walls, brightly lit to enhance the colors of Rory's work.

"She seems easy to please," said Rory.

"Only when things are going her way." She chuckled and cleared her throat. "So, how was the rest of the festival after I left?"

Sadie wrinkled her nose as soon as she spoke. She'd never mastered the art of small talk. A more pressing question was on the tip of her tongue. Rory, ever the silent observer, saw through her pretense in a second, but the only hint was a quirk of a smile that disappeared as fast as Sadie caught it.

"You had your eye on these last night," Rory said, nodding toward the stained-glass animal ornaments dangling from a metal tree on the nearest table. "I bet Cara would like any one of them to hang in a window. The festival was great. I sold out of my new trees."

A bushy-tailed red fox had Cara written all over it. She'd always had a soft spot for their resident fox, Todd. Sadie slipped its gray, velvet ribbon from the branch at the same time she spotted a squirrel on the opposite side of the tree.

Hayes would love that. She smiled to herself as she pictured him unwrapping it and exchanging a look with her at their shared joke. The squirrel incident on the day they'd first met was definitely one to remember.

"She'll like that one, too," Rory said as Sadie detached it from a branch.

She stood quietly at the counter while Rory encased them in bubble wrap. After Rory tucked the ornaments safely inside the bag and handed it over, Sadie pinned Rory with a look.

"I didn't come here only to Christmas shop," she started.

Rory smiled wryly. "I figured."

"Do you and Hayes know each other?"

Rory came around from behind her counter and leaned against it.

"Sort of. Couldn't for the life of me remember his name until you introduced us, though." Rory laughed, but then her brow furrowed. "You don't remember, do you? Hayes and I met on a blind date like fifteen years ago."

An envious knot twisted her middle. She pushed aside the knowledge of Hayes and her best friend together and hoped her smile hid the surprise at this revelation.

Sadie shook her head. "How would I have remembered that?"

"Because you were there. And it was the strangest date I'd ever had." Rory crossed her arms. "If he was any less interested in me, we would have been sworn enemies."

Confused, Sadie looked down at the floor, trying to piece together the memory.

"Of course you don't remember," Rory assured her, taking her hand. "It was such a bad time for you."

Sadie wracked her brain trying to conjure up an image of Hayes and Rory together.

Rory dropped her hand.

"A friend of Hayes arranged everything, from meeting that night at the festival to getting drinks afterward," Rory said. "I think it was the place in Rock Island that has the patio overlooking the river."

"Diablo's on the River." It was starting to come back. Evan had clung possessively to her hand all night, while hitting on someone else.

Rory snapped her fingers. "Yes."

"There were six of us, right?" Evan kept ogling another other guy's date, even going so far as to compliment her a few times in front of everyone. Sadie could still taste the bitter humiliation. "Evan was an even bigger jerk that night than usual."

"But Hayes jumped to your defense, don't you remember?" Rory prompted. "Evan was being his jerk self, and Hayes called him out."

"How do you remember that so well?"

"I was a little embarrassed at the time. Here I was on a first date with this gorgeous guy, and he spent the rest of the night focused on you."

"He did?" She'd apparently blocked out much of the night. "I wonder why?"

"I asked him the same question later on that night after we'd all gone our separate ways. He said your husband was trash. He shouldn't have treated you that way."

Sadie chuckled. "Boy, wasn't that an understatement."

It'd taken months to change her mindset from one of survival to recovery after she let go of their marriage. But while she was in the thick of it, she'd been held hostage in Evan's orbit, unable to see life beyond that point. How had she been so blind to everything else outside of that relationship? Thank goodness for her family's and Rory's support that had helped her navigate her way through it.

"But why would he do that?" she asked again, still fuzzy with the details surrounding Hayes's attentiveness.

Sympathy wrinkled Rory's forehead. "I don't know. At the time I thought it was odd, too. But maybe it was the first sign," she said with a shrug.

"Of what?"

"That you belong together? Who knows."

Sadie laughed awkwardly as a tingle crawled up her arms. Rory's words stole her breath for a few seconds. "Now you're branching out from glassmaking into fiction."

Rory lifted a shoulder. "All is fair in love and art."

# Chapter Thirty

Sadie had spent a harried few days knocking off items from her to-do list in preparation for Christmas and Cara's recovery time when she'd be short-handed. The animals would get their usual attention—meals, dressing changes, and medication—but she'd hoped to take it a little easier between Christmas and New Year's Day. Cara and Hayes had worked in tandem to help, but Cara's mind was preoccupied. She wasn't her usual upbeat self.

Cara arrived home from her outpatient surgery on Wednesday that week. She stirred on the couch later that afternoon, across the room from where Sadie sat reading her book. Sadie was beside her in a moment with a cup of water. She angled the straw toward Cara so she wouldn't have to lift her head from the pillow.

"How are you feeling?"

Cara sipped, then relaxed against the pillow.

"Like I'm floating in a sea of cotton."

Sadie chuckled. "That good? How about your ankle?"

She raised her leg slightly, her lower limb bound with layers of gauze and elastic bandages. "I can't feel it. Yet."

"You should start using this contraption soon to keep the swelling down." She toed a box next to the couch holding a portable ice machine sent home with her from the hospital. "But Hayes said everything went well."

"Where is Hayes?"

Sadie swallowed, avoiding her eyes. She settled into the arm chair opposite the couch again. "He went to pick up your prescriptions."

"If it's pain meds, I'm not taking them. I like to feel how I'm healing."

"You might change your mind after whatever they gave you at the hospital wears off."

Cara wrinkled her nose. She brought the cup to her lips again and took another sip.

"You sound like Hayes. He lectured me on the way to the hospital about following doctor's orders. I think he's getting restless and wants to hurry the healing process so he can get out of town." Cara set the cup back on the coffee table.

Sadie crossed her arms and leaned forward. "I thought he liked it here. He's anxious to leave?"

"A little. He's always needed his space."

That uneasy feeling was back. It happened each time she thought of Hayes leaving Port Chance.

"Does he even have a place lined up in Des Moines yet?" Hayes hadn't mentioned anything, but she hadn't exactly asked, either.

"No, he won't make a commitment until he gets a feel for the job," Cara said with her eyes closed again. "It's so like him.

Always ready to move on." Her laugh was a low rumble in her throat.

"Has he always been good about visiting? I mean, when he lived in Illinois?"

Cara's eyes popped open and her focus settled on Sadie.

"Yes, he's better than I would be." A one-sided smile transformed her sleepy expression. "Don't worry. This isn't the last you'll see of Hayes."

Her pulse galloped to a faster beat. "I'm not worried. Just thinking about you and your parents. Des Moines is more than twice as far as his last job."

"Sadie." Cara cocked her head and flashed a sympathetic look. "You can stop trying to fool me."

"Fool you?"

Cara nodded. "I haven't seen you so focused on anything else—or rather, anyone else—other than the shelter since I've met you. I mean, he walks into a room and it's almost painful to watch you struggle *not* to look at him."

Sadie couldn't bring herself to deny it.

Cara dropped her head against the pillow again. "Your secret is safe with me. But some secrets aren't meant to be kept."

"He's leaving. What's the point?"

Cara's eyes snapped open. "So you do have feelings for him. I knew it."

Sadie groaned in frustration.

The screen door creaked a warning before the front door pushed open. Hayes froze halfway through the door, his gaze flitting between the two of them.

"You look like you just walked into a ladies' Grecian bathhouse," Cara joked.

Hayes kicked off his boots on the mat. "Just surprised to see you awake."

"Sadie and I were just chatting." Cara looked pointedly at her before Sadie warned her with a firm glance about saying anything more.

She stood.

"Going so soon?" Cara said with a mischievous grin.

"I'm shopping for what I'm making for Christmas dinner."

As soon as the words came out of her mouth, Sadie regretted it. Reminding Hayes of his Christmas dinner invite to her parents' house wasn't a topic she wanted to bring up now, not with Cara smirking in the background. She trusted Cara not to divulge her newfound knowledge, but that didn't mean Sadie's comfort level wasn't suffering.

"Take it easy." She pointed to the bag of medications on the table. "And don't be a martyr. There's no sense in suffering."

Cara snorted with a quick look at Hayes before she settled her sights on Sadie again.

"Maybe you should take your own advice," Cara said.

Mowdry's Market was mayhem that afternoon, two days before Christmas. The small grocery store stocked what Sadie needed to make dinner rolls and the chocolate cherry pie, but weaving through the crowded aisles took every ounce of her patience. She crossed off molasses on her grocery list, added the jar into her basket, then headed toward the checkout.

She joined the end of a line six shoppers deep, switching the basket to her other arm when her muscles started aching.

"Merry Christmas, Sadie."

The voice caught Sadie off guard.

She turned to find Adelia Goodwin and her father standing there. Ever since Adelia helped move Jumpin' John from his palatial but empty family home into the renovated living space inside his shop down the street, Sadie hadn't seen much of Adelia. Still, they were long-time family friends.

"Thank you," she said. "What are you two up to for the holiday?"

Adelia looked at her father. "I'm bringing Dad back to Rock Island with me tonight. He'll stay with us through Christmas."

"Did you like that gift from your beau?" Jumpin' asked.

"Beau?" Sadie knew Jumpin's quirky personality well. His metaphors were well-known around town—he was quoted often—so an off-the-wall question didn't surprise her.

"The star. Said it was for the shelter. He talked about you like you two were an item."

Adelia gave her dad a look like he overstepped often.

"No, not my beau. He's just a friend." Everyone seemed to be more in tune to her feelings than she was at the moment.

"My mistake. Any time a man buys a lady friend something like that, I hope for the best."

Sadie couldn't imagine the direction of the conversation between Hayes and Jumpin', but it must not have been too crazy if Hayes hadn't brought it up. On the other hand, Jumpin's nosiness might have veered off the rails, embarrassing Hayes enough that he kept mum.

"Your friend had a look about him when he told me where that star would end up. Mentioned something about it being the North Star."

"Oh? And what look was that?" Sadie asked while her head buzzed with this knowledge about Hayes.

"*Lovestruck.*"

"Dad," Adelia said in a fierce whisper.

"What? You think I'm over-romanticizing again?" Jumpin' swept off a tweed cap to rub his bald head underneath.

"That's an understatement," Adelia said. "But also not minding your own business."

"I'm not prodding," he insisted. "And true romance is such a rare thing these days, Dellie. I appreciate young love for what it is."

"But she's already told you they're friends," Adelia said. She placed a hand on Sadie's arm. "I'm sorry."

Her face flamed. Even if this romance was just a figment of Jumpin's imagination, she felt it was obvious to anyone who looked twice at her lately.

"Don't worry about it," Sadie said, forcing a laugh. "He's moving on at the end of the month." As if that would cut any further speculation short where Jumpin' was concerned. She should know better.

"Ahh." He waggled a crooked finger at her. "Absence makes the heart—"

"*Dad*! Would you behave?" Adelia scolded.

"I'd better quit before she deposits me back at home," Jumpin' teased. "Merry Christmas to you and the rest of the Wendells."

Sadie wished them a Merry Christmas too as they found another checkout aisle. She paid, bagged her groceries, then dodged cars in the parking lot as she made her way to her own vehicle. Behind the wheel, she turned on the engine. The first song that blared from the speakers was Mariah Carey belting out the first stanza of "All I Want for Christmas" off the holiday playlist Janie had made for her, Kit, and Rose last year.

Slowly, she shook her head in resignation and chuckled. The universe was sending her sign after sign, a series of cosmic one-two punches from all directions lately. It wasn't a matter of knowing what she wanted anymore. It was how she'd get what she needed.

# Chapter Thirty-One

No matter how many reasons Hayes used on Cara to get out of the Wendell Christmas dinner, his sister countered with a point about why he should go.

He'd made the two of them a casserole and coffee cake for Christmas breakfast, and then they'd exchanged gifts, all the while debating about the dinner later that afternoon.

"You're not *listening* to me," she'd said. "You need to be there."

"I hear you loud and clear, Cara, but this is decidedly a bad idea. You shouldn't be alone, especially today of all days."

"I don't know how I can be any more clear, without spelling it out for you," she countered. When he looked across the table at her, she'd bugged her eyes out at him while spooning a bite of casserole into her mouth. "Missing this Christmas dinner could have a direct impact on your *life*."

"Now you're just being dramatic."

No doubt Rory had spilled the ugly details to Sadie after the festival. He wouldn't blame Rory for embellishing his leading role in the worst date of her life, and Sadie, being the kind, loyal friend she was, would only commiserate now that Rory helped jog her memory. If Sadie wanted nothing to do with him before, that miserable night sealed his fate for good. It was the best reason, at least as good as any other, to steer clear of the Wendell Christmas dinner.

But instead of standing his ground, Hayes added another shirt to the pile of rejected Christmas dinner attire accumulating on the futon, finally beaten down by Cara's persistence. He had thirty minutes to figure out what to wear before heading to the Wendells'. Thirty minutes suddenly felt like three. Panic was setting in.

"What's wrong with that one?" Cara asked as a plum corduroy, button-down shirt floated onto the others.

"It pulls too much across my chest."

"That might not be such a bad thing," she quipped, waggling a brow. "You never know whose eye you'll catch."

"First of all, the only Wendell woman not already taken isn't interested in me, so I'm pretty sure a shirt isn't going to work any magic. Secondly, wearing a too-small shirt is a decidedly bad idea because I'm going to overeat like I usually do."

"Oh, good point," she said, pushing out her stomach. "*Pop, pop!*"

"Funny. You can go back to your room any time now."

She huffed. "And miss all the fun?"

He shook out another sweater from his chest of drawers, a forest-green weave with a dark-red stripe across the chest. It had potential.

"That looks festive," Cara said.

He slipped it on only to discover a hole near the hem.

"Think they'll notice?" he asked, sticking his finger through it. "I could tuck this side in."

"No one tucks sweaters into their pants. They'll think you forgot to straighten yourself when you came out of the bathroom."

He peeled that one off too with a loud groan.

"I had no idea you're so picky when it comes to your wardrobe. Just close your eyes and wear the next one you pull out of your drawer."

*What do I have to lose?*

He squeezed his eyes shut and sifted around the drawer. His hand closed around another sweater. Holding it against his chest, he opened his eyes.

Cara hooted.

"I *dare* you to wear that."

The ugly sweater he'd bought for an office party a few years ago was covered in reindeer faces with pom-pom noses. Sadly, he hadn't even earned the "ugliest sweater" title for it after counting on being a shoo-in for the top prize.

"You couldn't pay me enough to put this on again. I don't even know why I still have it." He stuffed it back into the drawer and pulled the plum corduroy shirt off the pile. "I'll just go with this."

"Good choice. It enhances your dark and dangerous looks."

"My what?"

"Has anyone ever mentioned you look like a more rugged version of Timothy Dalton's James Bond?"

He shrugged on the shirt again. "You're too much."

"I'm serious."

"I need to go." He grabbed his keys and the holiday arrangement for Sonya from the table.

"Have fun. And don't forget the utensils rule: work your

way from the outside in," Cara said as she rearranged her foot propped on a pillow.

He rolled his eyes. "I don't think the Wendells are that fancy."

Cara put her finger up. "And remember to get two napkins, if possible. One to place on your lap, and one for your fingers near your plate."

"You're making me feel like a Neanderthal."

She shrugged. "When the shoe fits...and don't forget my doggy bag."

"Sadie would never let me leave without one." He was running late. His keys and the hostess gift already in hand, he just needed his coat by the door.

"Ahem." Cara cleared her throat.

Hayes stopped on his way to the door and turned.

Cara pointed to him then her own shirt. "Looking a little too sexy for the day, big brother."

Hayes glanced down at his shirt. With one too many buttons undone, half of his bare chest was exposed. Cara collapsed against the couch pillows with laughter.

"I should have let you go like that," she said.

"I'm so lucky to have a sister who entertains herself at my expense." He buttoned the last two buttons.

"Correction: you're so lucky to have a sister who *cares*." She shooed him to the door with her hands. "Love you. Have fun."

The star-littered sky was clear except for a stray cloud that filtered out the moon for a minute as he drove to the Wendells' house. A small fleet of cars was parked haphazardly along the winding pea gravel drive leading up to the house when he pulled in a few minutes later. As soon as he found a space, he grabbed the arrangement and hurried to the front door. His pulse kept time with his footsteps, a maddening beat in his head.

"Hayes!" Rose exclaimed as the door flew open. "Look who it is, everyone! Hayes is here!"

Rose gripped his arm, pulling him into the house as the Wendell women converged in the foyer, a bustling, noisy welcome party. Aaron Wendell hung back with an apologetic smile as if to say some things were out of his control.

*But where is Sadie?*

"How's Cara?" Kit asked.

"Has it started to snow yet?" Janie asked.

Rose let go of his arm to re-tie her apron springs. "I hope you like mashed potatoes because Mom made double the usual amount."

"Double?" Sonya piped in, coming down the hall. "Try triple."

Janie clucked. "Don't put him on the spot. Maybe he hates potatoes."

Questions flew at him as Janie took over for Rose by guiding him farther into the house. Kit took the table arrangement from him and presented it to Sonya, who cooed over the faux snow-dusted pine boughs, cardinals, and pine cones artfully arranged in the willow basket. Kudos to Cara for thinking of it, something he would have overlooked. He'd thank her again later if he survived the dinner.

They led him down a hallway in a cacophony of conversation, questions, and interruptions. He had no choice but to turn a corner since they surrounded him like they were his personal security detail, bringing him into a bright, spacious kitchen with an island as big as a king-sized bed.

Sadie stood at the island slicing fresh green beans. She glanced up to lock eyes with him.

"Merry Christmas, Hayes," she said quietly.

Despite the conversations buzzing in his ears, Hayes wasn't surprised her voice carried. Time froze as he took in the sight of her. Sadie wore a thigh-length gold velvet shirt over black leggings, and black boots which made her the tallest of her sisters at the moment. She'd pinned back her hair with a simple black rhinestone barrette on one side. It accentuated the angles of her face and her wide-set eyes. He took a deep, uneven breath. At least she was still talking to him. A good sign.

He approached the counter, pulling up a stool. Her sisters scattered to different spots in the room to continue prepping food.

"What was Cara doing when you left?" she asked. Her forehead wrinkled.

"Giving me etiquette lessons, even as I headed out the door."

Wide-eyed, she waited to see if he joked, then burst out laughing.

"She's good at giving advice, isn't she?" Sadie said when her laughter died.

"The best." He looked at the countertop separating them. "What can I do?"

"Just sit there and keep her company," Kit piped in from across the room.

Sadie ducked her head, renewing her focus on the beans.

"Hayes, congratulations on the job. Sadie filled us in before you got here," Rose said as she stood at the stove. "Des Moines has a lot to offer."

"I don't know...I've grown used to small-town life," he said.

"It does have its advantages," Kit said. "But the gossip is what gets me."

Janie cracked up at that. "That's because you give everyone so much to talk about."

He kept his eyes on Sadie throughout the whole exchange. Her brow furrowed every time one of them spoke up. As Kit and Janie quibbled, Sadie's mouth grew tighter.

"Maybe you should go keep my dad company," Sadie finally said in a hushed tone. "You know, if this is too much. He and Mark are watching the game."

When he didn't move, Sadie looked up. Her brows arched as if she meant, *What are you waiting for?*

"I'm happy right here if that's okay with you."

Sadie gave him a small, resigned nod. Silently, she cut the last of the beans, added some spices, then tossed them around in the bowl. When she lined the baking sheet with foil, he was there with the bowl to dump them onto the pan. They made sure the beans were evenly spaced, pushing them around with their fingers. Their fingers brushed together a few times, spiking his pulse. Across from him, Sadie continued separating the beans, keeping her attention on task.

That was his cue.

He should have followed his gut.

He should have stood his ground with Cara.

He hated thinking Sadie's discomfort was his fault. She should be spending time with her family on Christmas, not being forced to interact with him.

Hayes mumbled his intentions to join her dad and future brother-in-law after all in the other room and slid off the stool before he noticed her reaction, if there was one at all.

Her stiff, silent mood told him one thing clearly: Sadie wished he'd stayed home.

# Chapter Thirty-Two

As lively conversation bounced from one subject to another around the dinner table an hour later, Sadie forced smile after smile and laughed on cue. Inside though, her chest ached with despair. She wished she could pretend all was well, but Hayes's impending move crushed her spirits, especially as the topic came up again and again since Hayes had arrived.

"How far is Des Moines, anyway?" Rose asked. She'd been born a homebody. Running Apple Hill Farm didn't afford much travel, so Rose wasn't the greatest at geography.

*Two hours and twenty-eight minutes—176 miles.*

Hayes set down his fork. "About two and a half hours."

"Oh, that's not bad." Rose's eyes flitted to hers.

"There's a nice orchard operation north of town," Jordan said. "I've met the owners on occasion at conferences."

"An orchard visit would make for a nice afternoon activity for you and Cara if she came to visit," Mom said with a quick glance in Sadie's direction. "Or anyone else for that matter."

Sadie stabbed at her sweet potato casserole, vowing to give them both an earful when they had a private moment.

Kit regaled everyone with her new idea for themed boat rides next spring. A long discussion followed about the new boat landing under construction in Davenport, with easy access to the historic district. Janie's fiancé, Mark, had the inside scoop.

Seconds were passed around the table. The clinking of utensils cut into the conversation for a few minutes until plates were refilled.

"Sadie," Rose said, "Tyler told me this year's school fundraiser earned more than in years past with the rescue as their charity of choice. Is that true?"

Sadie dabbed at the corner of her mouth with a napkin and nodded.

"That's what Heidi said when she called with the news. The donations and a check were delivered yesterday."

"Merry Christmas to *you*," Kit said.

"Right? I haven't been able to sort through everything yet, but it's a huge relief to not have to live week to week anticipating needs."

"Hayes, when will you be leaving town?" Mom asked.

"Not until New Year's Day, so I've got another full week," he said with a fleeting glance in Sadie's direction.

Was there an epidemic of let's-keep-looking-at-Sadie going around? Her face hadn't stopped burning since Rose asked about the distance to Des Moines.

"Thank goodness. Sadie could probably use the help with Cara being out of commission."

Hayes looked just as cornered as she felt.

"That's my intention," he said simply. "I'm at her disposal with whatever she needs."

Sonya made the rounds at the table with a water pitcher, followed by Kit with the wine bottle. When Sonya emptied the pitcher before more glasses were filled, Sadie held out her hand.

"I can get more water. I'm finished eating anyway." She choked on the last word. Everyone's attention flitted down toward their end of the table.

In the kitchen, she caught a sliver of her reflection in the stainless steel microwave at eye level. She didn't need a full mirror to interpret her painfully pinched expression. Every word from Hayes added an extra weight to her heart.

As she came back into the dining room, she paused mid-step when she caught part of the conversation between Rose and Hayes who were seated next to each other and closest to the door.

"...needs to get out more," Rose said. "All she does is work, then she goes home to that lonely cabin. All by herself out there in the woods? She needs to have a little fun."

"I've never gotten the impression that Sadie's lonely," Hayes said.

"Oh, she'd definitely tell you she's not." Rose leaned closer to Hayes, but whispered loudly enough that Sadie—and anyone else paying attention—could hear. "Maybe she could use a night out while you're still in town."

Sadie gasped. Rose and Hayes shifted in their seats.

Mortified, Sadie set the water pitcher on the table and hurried out of the room.

"Sadie," Rose called.

She couldn't go back in that room, not with Rose feeding

Hayes advice about how he should come to her rescue. Hayes shouldn't have come to dinner for this very reason. She'd hoped to navigate Hayes's last week in Port Chance with peace of mind, with the knowledge that people came into and out of her life for a reason. Not everyone stayed, not even someone who'd stirred something inside her that she believed she'd never feel again.

As she rushed down the hallway to the front door, she listened for footsteps. *His* footsteps. She desperately hoped he'd come into her life and would decide to stay.

# Chapter Thirty-Three

Hayes closed the front door behind him and found Sadie at the far end of the wide front porch, facing away from him. The wood floor creaked underneath his boots as he walked the length of the porch, which echoed in the otherwise peaceful night.

"Sadie."

"You're going to miss getting a helping of my chocolate cherry pie," she said lightly, turning to watch him make his way over to where she stood. "Kit always goes for seconds before Mom finishes serving firsts."

He came up alongside her and gripped the porch railing, looking out over the snow-draped lawn. An owl hooted close by. The evening landscape looked beautiful, lit by a slice of moon peeking out from behind a cloud. Light caressed Sadie's face, which made her appear wistful and at peace, despite being subjected to the embarrassing episode inside.

"I'll take my chances. I thought you might need some company."

She chuckled. "As much as I love my family, they're a little much sometimes."

"I'm sorry you had to hear that," he said.

Sadie let out another humorless chuckle. "It's par for the course. Rose is a mother hen. She thinks everyone is in need of her help. But she's right. I've lived alone for too long."

"But if you're happy, that's all that matters."

The corner of her eye crinkled with a smile. "I'm not sure that I am anymore."

"No?" Her nearness took his breath away.

"There's more to life than...than what I spend my time on."

This didn't sound like the passionate, fiercely focused woman he'd met the first time he walked into the rescue. She sounded like someone at a crossroads, struggling with which path to take.

"What happened to your North Star?"

Sadie cocked her head at him with a smile that fanned the embers in his heart. "I think I've lost sight of it, at least temporarily."

"What are we going to do about it?"

Her eyes widened, searching his. Then she abruptly faced the lawn again as if she couldn't bear to look at him a second longer.

He studied her profile. Her expression was a blank slate except for the tick on her jawline illuminated by the porch light.

He loved her. It was that simple.

But it wasn't that simple, because what did loving Sadie Wendell leave him with if she didn't feel the same way? A broken heart, that's what.

He leaned his elbows on the railing to look out at the lawn again. The owl, probably spotting prey, rustled the pine boughs in a tree overhead as it took flight. Its outspread wings cast a shadow over the lawn as it swooped down from its perch to land in another tree out of sight.

Sadie held her breath. He knew this because the evenly timed puffs from her soft exhales stopped.

When she spoke again, her voice was softer.

"Ever since you walked into the rescue in October, I've been trying to figure out how I knew you."

*Uh oh. Here it comes.*

"You remember, don't you?" she asked.

"I didn't until I saw Rory again at the festival."

"She told me about the blind date," she added. "That there were six of us out that night. Even listening to her version, the details are still fuzzy to me. I think I've just completely blocked out a lot of my life from back then."

Hayes straightened. "I was such a jerk to her. I'm not even going to bother with the excuse that I was young and stupid. My behavior was just wrong by all accounts."

Sadie turned to him again. Her hand rested on the railing, a fingertip away from his arm. He wanted to take it so badly he could taste the desire on his tongue.

"But she also said she'd never seen someone so concerned for someone he didn't know. Someone so desperately in need of a kindness." Sadie turned to face him. "I *was* desperate, and you were there."

He swallowed noisily and nodded.

"I wish I could've carried that memory with me all these years. Then I might not feel like I'm losing something I just found," she said, choking on the last word.

"I'm not following." His heartbeat thudded to a stop.

"I don't want you to go, Hayes."

What little breath he'd been holding left his body as he closed the space between them, wrapping his arm around her shoulders and drawing her to him. He cradled her face in his other hand, pulling her gaze upward so he could look into her eyes, searching for signs that this was a dream.

"I don't want to go, either."

"Then don't," she said in a hush. Her lips grazed his mouth.

"If you really mean that, Sadie..."

But he read the look in her eyes, and that was all it took for him to kiss her like he'd wanted to for weeks. Sadie melted against him with a sigh, pushing her fingers into his hair at the back of his neck, bringing him deeper into the kiss. His head spun with pent-up desire, and despite their proximity to her family's Christmas festivities happening on the other side of the wall, letting her go seemed next to impossible.

If he woke up in the morning with the realization that Sadie told him not to leave Port Chance, knowing for certain this wasn't a dream or a figment of his imagination, then he'd do everything in his power to make sure he didn't.

# Chapter Thirty-Four

Balancing on a ladder, Sadie took the last bundle of bedding from Hayes and stuffed it onto the top shelf inside the closet a few days after Christmas. The two closets in the intake building were crammed to the gills with the donations gifted to the rescue by Sycamore Elementary. The extra supplies would give them a cushion as Sadie waited for more donations to roll in along with the approval of a much-anticipated state grant.

Hayes held onto her hand as she navigated her way down the ladder. Before she could take the last step onto the floor, he pulled her toward him so she landed in his arms.

"Taking advantage of my vulnerable position, huh?" She looped her arms around his neck while he held her off the floor.

"Tell me you don't want to be here and I'll put you down." He gazed up into her face with hooded eyes.

Sadie bit down on her lip, stifling a laugh.

"That's what I thought," he teased.

Hayes released her and she slid to the floor, but she kept her hands locked behind his head. Now that their feelings for each other had aligned, Sadie wasn't letting him get too far away.

Cara, for one, was over the moon.

*It's about time you two discovered what everyone else in the world knew all along,* Cara texted her after Hayes came home from Christmas dinner that night to report the news. Cara was quick to take credit for convincing Hayes to come for dinner in the first place.

Across the room, Katie the groundhog ran a frenzied lap around her cage, startling them.

"She looks like she's healed nicely," Hayes said with a chuckle. "When do you plan on releasing her?"

She walked over to Katie's cage, delighted that the animal had made a full recovery.

"Not until the spring. Groundhogs hibernate, so it's too late for her to find decent shelter."

Hayes folded the ladder and set it next to the door to return to the equipment shed.

"I'm sure she doesn't mind the extended stay at Sadie's Spa," he said.

She giggled. "I have heated towels and spring water, but she'll be disappointed to learn I no longer offer hot stone massages."

"That's a shame," he said with a mock frown. "I guess I'll have to take Furever Friends Rescue off the designated charity list now for the company I'll be working for. That's over eight hundred potential donors who might be groundhog advocates."

"Hayes, really? The rescue is on a charity list? This is a huge first!"

"Really. Cara suggested it, so it wasn't all me. I filled out the forms today."

"That's amazing!" She threw her arms around him again, but pulled back. "Wait, why would employees at a Des Moines plant care to designate matching funds for a little non-local charity?"

"Not Des Moines. I'm talking about the Muscatine facility."

Her jaw dropped. A spot of hope blossomed. "Did you ask to be transferred?" she whispered.

"I did."

"And?"

"I'll hear by the end of the week."

She squealed, hugging Hayes so tightly he let out an involuntary groan.

"Keep this up and I'll have to retire early," he said, drawing her closer for a kiss. "Then you'll never get rid of me."

Sadie savored the soft, gentle way his mouth covered hers until she felt him smiling. Then she playfully tugged his bottom lip with her teeth. He was such a delightful tease.

"That would not be a problem."

## Epilogue – Ten Months Later

Golden oak leaves fluttered down along with the occasional *plunk* of an acorn, landing on the driveway around Sadie and Hayes as they folded up the last table outside the carriage house.

"I'd say today was a hit," Hayes said. He offered to take the table after securing the latch, but she held onto her end.

"I'm glad I wasn't the only one here. I hate feeling like I'm under a microscope during these events. Thank you for helping."

Hayes threw his head back with a hearty laugh. He walked the length of the table to where she stood, placed his hands on her face, and drew her in for a kiss.

"Succeed together, fail together. Is that our motto now?" he asked.

She grinned against his lips as a pleasurable ripple tickled her spine. No matter how many times he kissed her, it was always a soul-shivering thrill.

"I'm better than I used to be. I never would've taken an interview before I met you."

"Love and bravery must go hand in hand," he said. Hayes threaded his fingers through her hand as he dropped them from her face.

The first fall open house for the shelter, meticulously organized by Cara, had been a success. Sadie had counted two hundred people before noon milling around the area they'd designated for the celebration. Cara had connected with some local vendors—Kit's friend, Ginger Giatti's mobile pet rescue-inspired coffee truck, a T-shirt vendor, a dog biscuit bakery, and others. A balloon artist dazzled the kids with animal shapes. Hayes had served cake.

When a local news station had come to interview Sadie amid the festivities, she hadn't felt half as nervous as she expected, thanks to Hayes standing in the background.

"Let's lock up here, then head down to the intake building," Sadie said. "I need to change the dressing on the opossum before we move the new swing into the raccoon enclosure."

After they'd stored the tables inside the carriage house, they walked hand in hand down the foliage-strewn driveway. Todd the fox paced in his enclosure. A female fox, recently introduced to the same space as Todd and Flora, stood still while keeping a wary eye on her and Hayes.

When she'd told Cara to post a short list of needs on their social media site, a new bamboo seat, part of an old chair someone no longer needed, had arrived that morning. The speed at which donations flooded the shelter still surprised her. Their network had grown even more over the last year, thanks to Cara's engaging posts.

Hayes had taken a more active role in the shelter over the summer, too, when his work schedule eased. As soon as he'd signed on to work at the Muscatine plant, his supervisor had confided that he'd dodged a bullet. Hours were longer in Des Moines, and that department wasn't as well-organized as the closer option.

Sadie unlocked the door of the intake building and her attention was immediately drawn to the box sitting by itself in the middle of the exam table.

"What's this?"

Her heart hammered as she noted the size of the box. It couldn't be. Her face flamed. Sadie hoped someday that it might come to this, but so soon? Was she ready to say "yes"?

"A little something," Hayes said. "You've always insisted on no gifts, that you like experiences instead, but I saw this and knew you'd love it."

"Yeah?" She couldn't manage to get rid of the lump in her throat.

He nodded. "Trust me." His eyes crinkled with delight.

She peeled wrapping paper from one end, then the other, taking her time. A gold box peeked through when she tore the rest of the paper away. Hayes watched her, his mouth curved with a gentle smile.

"Hayes..."

"Just open it."

She swallowed as she lifted the lid. Nestled into the cotton square lining was a gilded gold star. Cut from wood and painted with a dainty filagree design, the ornament was threaded with a translucent gossamer ribbon. She plucked it from the box, letting it dangle by the ribbon as the gold glinted from the over-head lights.

"Hayes, it's *beautiful*."

He'd stepped closer while she admired his gift. As Hayes

took the box from her and set it on the side table, then took her hand, her attention shifted from the star to his face.

"Remember when I hung that star over the shelter door? That was as much for me as it was a symbol for you," he said, his voice husky with emotion.

She clutched the ornament to her chest when he pulled her closer. "What do you mean?"

"You're my North Star, Sadie. Wherever you are, that's where I want to be."

Sadie choked back the sensation in her throat. She wasn't a crier, but it was a lot harder to swallow at the moment. And her eyes, why was her vision blurry? Had she suddenly come down with seasonal allergies? *Silly*. But she couldn't hold back a laugh and it came out way too loud and high-pitched, and that made her laugh even more.

Her cheeks burned from smiling so hard. "I can't imagine being anywhere other than with you."

"Do you think you'll feel the same way a year from now?" he implored.

She nodded. "Definitely."

"Two years from now?"

"More than that."

He slipped something from his jacket pocket. "Like, twenty years from now? Forty?"

She followed the movement of his hand and guessed what it was before he knelt in front of her, snapping open the lid.

The moistness in her eyes spilled over into a single tear that trailed down her cheek.

"Forever," she said, kneeling too because she needed to be close to him.

Hayes cradled her face as he kissed her. It was gentle at first, but an urgency grew like a runaway brush fire, and she found herself clinging to him like he was both the kindling to keep it burning and the only way to quench it.

Cara burst into the room then and skidded to a stop as they hurriedly pretended that she hadn't just caught them kissing.

"Shame on me. I'll just back out of here," Cara mumbled with a barely contained smile, reversing her course through the door again.

"Don't be ridiculous. Get in here," said Hayes, pulling her by the hand into the room.

"You're the first to hear," Sadie said. She thrust her hand toward Cara who took a few extra seconds to register what had just happened.

"You're *engaged*? You guys!"

"Don't act so surprised," she said. "You've had a hand in this from the beginning."

"And thank goodness for that! Someone needed to take the initiative, or we wouldn't be standing here right now." Cara clasped her hands underneath her chin, giving them a moony look. "Wait, I need to preserve the moment!" She patted her coat pockets and pulled out her phone.

"I'd better not see this in a post before our families hear from us personally," Hayes warned. He pulled Sadie close as she fanned her fingers to show off the ring for Cara's impromptu engagement photo.

When Cara left with the excuse of having to pull something out of the oven, Hayes swooped her into his arms again.

"Do you really think Cara will keep this a secret before we tell everyone?" he asked.

Sadie nodded. "She has a good track record."

He chuckled. "What's that supposed to mean?"

"She knew I had a thing for you well before Christmas last year."

He squinted at her as a mischievous smile transformed his lips. "You played a mean game of hard to get."

"I've happily lost that game." Hayes's kiss drew the goose-bumps out on her arms.

"So you have," he said.

# A Special Note to Readers

Thank you so much for reading *Christmas in Port Chance*. I hope you loved Sadie and Hayes's love story as much as I enjoyed writing it. There's a prequel story to the series, *Meet Me in Port Chance*, that you'll enjoy for free when you join my newsletter Welcome to the Sweet Life. You'll also get access to other free content as well as subscriber-only giveaways and new story sneak peeks.

And, if you enjoyed the book, I'd love for you to leave a review on Amazon and/or Goodreads.

# Happy Reading!

*Dawn*

# Acknowledgments

First, I'd like to recognize all of the amazing wildlife rehabilitation specialists out there who do such inspiring work to support the animals that come under their care. Three rehabbers in particular inspired Sadie's work in this book: Raccoon Ridge Rehab, Illinois Raptor Center and Oaken Acres Wildlife Center. Rehabbing can be an exhausting, painful, and heartbreaking mission some days, but some of the stories I've heard of healing and release are truly magical and uplifting.

Much appreciation goes to my editor Sarah West and her keen eye for my errant commas and other inconsistencies in the manuscript. She's always so patient with my "just one more week" requests to extend the deadline. She's been so wonderful to work with on this series.

To my dear fellow writer and friend, Rachael Bloome, for reading early chapters of this manuscript, sometimes at a moment's notice. I so appreciate her amazing and heartfelt advice and support for my writing.

Many thanks to Mary Ellen Cox for catching the pesky

things that have slipped under the radar until the last minute before publication.

Thank you to designer extraordinaire Wilette Cruz for another stunning Port Chance cover.

And finally, my family, who is my constant source of strength and inspiration. I love you all.

# About the Author

D.E. Malone writes contemporary small-town romance and is the author of the Hearts in Hendricks, Blueberry Point Romance, and Port Chance series. Her work has appeared in the Chicken Soup for the Soul series, *Highlights for Children*, and other publications. When not writing, she loves outdoors—gardening, hiking, and exploring places off-the-beaten path. She lives in central Illinois with her husband.

Follow her at Facebook https://www.facebook.com/dmalonebooks

Follow her at Instagram https://www.instagram.com/dmalonebooks